A BLAKE HARTE MYSTERY

SPOTLIGHT

ROBERT INNES

Copyright © 2017 Robert Innes
Cover designed by Ashley Mcloughlin

1st Edition: October 24th 2017

All rights reserved. This book or any portion thereof may not be reproduced or used in any manner whatsoever without the express written permission of the author except for the use of brief quotations in a book review.

All characters appearing in this work are fictitious. Any resemblance to real persons, living or dead is purely coincidental.

For questions and comments about this book, please contact the author at rgwisox@aol.com.

ISBN: 9781973191254
Imprint: Independently Published.

A BLAKE HARTE MYSTERY
BOOK 5

OTHER BLAKE HARTE BOOKS

Untouchable
Confessional
Ripples
Reach
Spotlight

SPOTLIGHT

HARRISON OPENED HIS EYES, BUT HE MAY AS well have kept them closed. All he could see was darkness. He felt groggy and confused, his head was throbbing, and he had a sharp pain in his back, as if there was something sticking into him.

He raised his head slowly and tried to look around him. Then, he realised that he was in an extremely confined space, and that his hands and feet were tied with, what felt like, thick rope. In the next second, he felt the unmistakable rise and fall of a car going over a bump of some kind in the road. Harrison's heart thumped loudly in his chest; he was in a car boot.

He began to feel extremely claustrophobic, his heart felt like it was going to burst out his chest. Panic overcame him. A cold sweat broke out on his forehead. He closed his eyes and thought back to a conversation he and Blake had had very early on in their relationship. Blake had taught him how to ease panic attacks and level himself so that whatever he was faced with, he could deal with more calmly and with more focus. Slowing his breathing, he kept his eyes shut and, despite his current situation, began to let the motion of the car journey rock him into a calmer state of mind. Once he began to feel his heartbeat lessen, he opened his eyes again and tried to look around him for any clue that could help him. He could feel that his mobile phone was no longer in his pocket, and he was finding it impossible to gauge what direction the car might be travelling in, and judging by the sound of the engine, they were picking up speed.

Harrison tried to recollect how he had ended up in this position. He had a vague memory of sitting down at the table with Blake, about to eat dinner. Then, he could just about picture a broom, a vacuum cleaner, and a mop bucket. After that, he was drawing a blank. The memories were there, but it was as if they were tantalisingly out of reach; shapes with no form as words with no meaning flew aimlessly around his mind.

Then, he heard the sound of the car speeding over gravel, and the bumping suddenly got worse. But then, as suddenly as the jolting had started, the car came to a sudden halt. The silence was amazing. Harrison did not know how long he lay there, unable to hear anything except his own shallow breathing before suddenly, the door of the boot flung open and he was blinded by the sunlight. Automatically, he went to shield his eyes, before remembering that his hands were out of action, leaving him just to squint up at the silhouette of his captor. Then, Harrison saw what they were holding. The outline in the sun was unmistakable. It was a gun.

"Oh good," said the figure. "You're awake. Move."

CHAPTER
ONE
TWO DAYS EARLIER

The roads on the outskirts of the village of Harmschapel were picturesque and quiet. In the midday sun, butterflies danced with each other in the air, and all that could be heard in the tranquil environment was the gentle sound of birds singing. But in the distance, the roar of a car engine could be heard, getting closer and closer. Suddenly, the peace was shattered as a crimson red car zoomed around a bend, with a police car not far behind.

In the passenger seat of the police car, Detective

Sergeant Blake Harte talked frantically into his radio. "We're on the roads outside of the village. Suspects are heading towards Clackton." There was a crackle of acknowledgment on the radio. "Come *on*, Michael! We're going to lose them!"

Sergeant Michael Gardiner glanced at him. "I am going as fast as I can. Unless you'd rather we ended up going flying into a field? I'm sure Angel would love that. Losing the suspects *and* writing off a car in the process. *They* know these roads. You can tell."

"*You* know these roads, don't you?" Blake exclaimed incredulously. "How do you normally get out of Harmschapel? Teleport?"

"It's not safe to do these bends at this speed," snapped Gardiner, frantically spinning the steering wheel to get them round a particularly sharp corner. "And *they* know it."

They were in pursuit of a car driven by two men that Harmschapel police had been trying to pin down for several months, on suspicion of drug dealing. Finally, that morning, they had caught them in the act of a transaction down a dark secluded street of Harmschapel, and Blake and Gardiner had given chase, leading them here.

The siren of the car wailed as they continued the pursuit. Blake inwardly cursed the location – if this had been happening in his old placement back in Sale near Manchester, they would have been able to cut them off via another road, but the winding country roads here were too narrow to even attempt to overtake them. All they could do until they reached a wider section was try and keep on their tail.

"Where the hell are they even going?" Blake asked. "There's nowhere for them to hide out here."

"You know these types," Gardiner grunted. "Desperate thugs will try anything to save their skin. And they know we've got enough evidence to get them both put away for a long time."

The road ahead went underneath a railway line, and instead of a bridge like in most residential areas, the road led them under the line via a small cramped tunnel, which curved in the middle. Blake remembered it from his first day arriving in Harmschapel, as he had to go through it fairly slowly because meeting any other traffic in the middle meant that one of the vehicles would have to reverse to let the other one through. It was certainly not safe to go through it at high speed, but nevertheless, that's exactly what they were doing. Blake felt his body tighten as they zoomed into the tunnel. The speed they were going, if there was any traffic coming the other way, there would certainly be a substantial accident. Fortunately, the road was clear and they were soon out in the bright sunshine again. But the car in front was now getting further ahead of them.

"We're losing them, Michael," Blake said sharply.

"Yes, I can see that!" snapped Gardiner, glaring at him. "Contrary to what you might believe, DS Harte, I am quite capable of –"

"*Michael, look out!*" shouted Blake.

Ahead of them, a large tractor was pulled out of the left hand side of a crossroad. Gardiner slammed on the brakes, and the car skidded across the road. It came to a stop, jolting them both forwards in their seats, inches from the end of the tractor's trailer. As it trundled across the lane in front of them, all they could do was watch the car they had been chasing disappear into the distance.

Blake slammed the dashboard with his fist. "*Dammit!*"

Gardiner sighed. "They must have seen the tractor and cut across it."

"I *hate* the countryside!" Blake fumed. "What am I supposed to tell Angel now?"

Gardiner shrugged. "That you lost them."

Blake's head spun round. "What do you mean *I* lost them? You were the one driving!"

Gardiner watched as the tractor finally cleared the road in front of them. By now, the other car would be miles ahead of them. "You're the commanding officer. I follow your orders. Technically, you were the one driving. I just steer."

Blake could only glare at him.

SPOTLIGHT

***

"Just let me do all the talking," Blake said to Gardiner as they walked into Harmschapel police station.

"That was my intention," Gardiner replied cheerfully, strolling past him.

Blake gritted his teeth but said nothing.

They walked into the meeting room, which was buzzing with activity. PCs Billy Mattison and Mini Patil were at their desks, tapping furiously on their computers, Sergeant Mandy Darnwood was talking on the telephone, and their new boss, Detective Inspector Jacob Angel, was sitting in his office, his tall skeletal frame giving him an unjust appearance of fragility and delicateness. He looked up, his cold blue eyes narrowing through his steel rimmed glasses as Blake and Gardiner approached his office door and knocked.

"Come in," he said sharply.

Blake took a deep breath and entered the office, Gardiner casually following behind.

"Ah, DS Harte," Angel said, placing his expensive looking pen down gently on the desk. "I take it this is to do with the arrests of the Pennines?"

Blake scratched the back of his head. He could just see the smug expressions on Keith Pennine and his son, James' faces when they had realised that they had escaped them. "Erm, no, Sir. I'm afraid not."

Angel raised a condescending eyebrow. "I see.

Would you care to tell me what happened?"

"They escaped, Sir," Blake replied. "We were in pursuit of them all the way up to the crossroads past Clifton Moore Tunnel, then a tractor got in the way, and they got away from us."

"And how, may I ask, was a tractor of all things allowed to get in your way?"

"It came out in front of us just as we were approaching the crossroads, Sir," Blake replied, glancing at Gardiner. "It was pulling a large trailer and because of the speed it was going, by the time it passed, they had long gone. Michael couldn't get 'round it in time."

"Michael couldn't? Why do you say that?"

Blake frowned. "I just meant because he was driving."

Angel clasped his hands together in front of him. "I see. That'll be all, Sergeant Gardiner."

Gardiner nodded and left the office with a slight look of smugness about him. Angel waited until the door to the office had been closed again and looked up at Blake. "DS Harte, how long have we been after the Pennines?"

"About four months."

"Indeed. Including two months where I was not here," Angel said calmly.

Blake's eyes narrowed as he tried to work out where this was going.

"And in that four months, as I understand it, they have always been one step ahead of us. Or, should I say, one step ahead of *you.*"

"Me?"

"You *have* been the person in charge of the investigation, have you not?"

Blake sighed. "Yes, Sir."

"And yet we still don't seem to have them. As I understand it, we don't even have a grasp on where they go when they're not on the street corners selling their drugs. They can't be far away, but they always seem to slip through our, or indeed, *your*, fingers."

It was taking Blake a considerable amount of effort not to tell Angel exactly what he could do with his condescending manner.

"Let me show you something," Angel said. He opened his large notebook and retrieved a pencil from a holder full of stationary in front of him. He wrote something in large letters before holding up the pad for Blake to read. "What does this say?"

Blake stared at the pad in disbelief. "It says *'DS Harte,'* Sir."

Angel nodded, then pulled out an erasure from the stationary pot and rubbed out something on the pad. He then held it up again. It now just read *'Harte.'*

"Two letters that were incredibly easy to get rid of," he said, just as calmly as ever. "I hope I've made my point. Now, if you could come in early tomorrow,

I'd be very grateful. I have something I wish to discuss with everybody. I'll see you at eight tomorrow, DS Harte. I just hope that is how I shall continue to regard you in the coming weeks."

Blake gave Angel an incredibly strained smile, and walked out of the office without another word.

CHAPTER
TWO

Life for Harrison Baxter had become almost utopian compared to a year ago. While his old life, living on his parents' farm, had been plagued with anxieties, and the general feeling that he was jumping at the sight of his own shadow, Blake's invitation to move in with him had made Harrison feel like a new person. Their relationship had gone from strength to strength, and it was finally starting to feel like he was putting the darkness of his life behind him at last.

Walking into the kitchen of Juniper Cottage, he

glanced at the clock. All being well, Blake would be home in about ten minutes. Harrison flicked the kettle on and glanced up at the calendar that was hanging from the cupboard. Blake had flipped the page onto a new month that morning. As he glanced at it, Harrison frowned as on the next day, Blake had written a name that Harrison did not recognise. *'Bethany.'* A scratching from the back door distracted him and he turned to see Betty the goat glaring at him through the window of the back door. Harrison sighed and walked towards the door, shaking his head. He had had Betty since he was a child, and he had made it clear to Blake when they had started their relationship that the goat was very much a part of his life. There had been times when she had been his only friend over the years and Harrison was not about to abandon her. Blake had accepted this but had been insistent that due to the amount of important paperwork he brought home from the police station, she could not be allowed to roam free in the house. The only one who had not been willing to agree with these conditions was Betty, who had previously been allowed free reign of Harrison's house and the property had had the damage to prove it. Her behaviour had been nothing short of obstinate the past couple of months, though she was slowly getting accustomed to her new surroundings.

Harrison opened the back door to entertain her for a few minutes when there was a sharp knock at the front door too. Harrison frowned. He was not expecting anybody, and it was very unlike Blake to have forgotten his keys. He opened the door and was surprised to see a woman and a man, both looking like they were in their sixties standing in front of him.

The woman raised her eyebrows as Harrison stared at her. She was wearing a frilly blouse, with perfectly coifed white hair, with a pair of glasses hanging down from her neck on a chain, and the man with her was rotund, greying at the sides, clutching two suitcases beneath his arms.

"Hello," Harrison said when it became clear the woman was not planning on speaking until he had. "Can I help you?"

"I'm not sure," the woman replied, looking Harrison up and down. "Who are you?"

"I'm Harrison," he replied. "I live here."

"Do you now?" she said, her eyes narrowing. "I see."

"Stephanie, love, will you get in?" the man hissed hastily. "These cases are giving my shoulder hell." He looked up at Harrison. "Look, can we come in, son?"

"We're looking for Blake," Stephanie said, ignoring the man who Harrison presumed was her husband. "We're his parents."

"Oh!" Harrison exclaimed. "Right! Yes. You better come in then."

"Much obliged," Stephanie said.

Harrison stepped aside and Stephanie stepped inside. "Do you want a hand with them?" he said to her husband, as he struggled with the cases.

"Aye, aye, thanks, lad," he said, thrusting a case in Harrison's direction. "Appreciate it, thanks. I'm Colin, by the way."

Once they were inside, Stephanie stood in the middle of the room and looked around. "So, where is he?"

"Blake?" Harrison said, closing the door behind Colin. "He's at work. Does he know you were coming?"

"No," Stephanie said, sitting down on the sofa, pushing the throw away from her distastefully.

"Oh, is it a surprise?"

"Aye, you could say that," Colin muttered, placing the cases down in the corner.

"Colin," Stephanie snapped, glancing at him.

"Yeah, yeah, alright," Colin said, standing up and groaning as he rubbed the small of his back. "Any chance of a cup of tea, lad? I'm parched after that drive. Listening to her attempts at map reading and trying to make your way round those roads on the way here is enough to drive any man mental."

Harrison glanced at Stephanie who either hadn't heard Colin's remark or had chosen to ignore it. "Yeah, of course, no problem," he said. "How do you have it?"

"Ah, you're a cracker. Milk, two sugars please," Colin smiled. "Her highness has it just with milk. Not too much though."

"Right," Harrison said nodding.

As he made the tea, Harrison realised that Blake had barely mentioned his parents. Harrison's family life was well known to Blake, him having arrested Harrison's parents, but he had remained strangely quiet on his own background. Just as he was stirring the milk into Stephanie's cup, Blake walked in, slamming the front door behind him.

"I have *had* it with that man!" he exclaimed, storming into the kitchen. "Jacob Angel is one of the biggest *arseholes* I have ever had the displeasure to meet!"

"Blake…" Harrison began.

"Today, me and Gardiner were pursuing this pair of drug dealers, and we lost them because Gardiner drives like Mr *bloody* Bean, and I get the blame!"

"Blake, listen, -"

"And he sits there, in his chair, like the sort of patronising, belittling, condescending, *stick insect* that he is, and do you know what he did? Wrote my name down and told me that, -"

"*Blake!*" Harrison exclaimed. "We've got company."

Blake frowned. "Who?" He turned to face the living room and his face dropped. "*Mother?*"

"Hello, Blake," Stephanie said, standing up.

"How are you, son?" Colin asked, more warmly.

Blake hugged his father, but the look of surprise in his face did not diminish. "What are you doing here?"

"Can we not drop in and see our own son now and again?" Stephanie asked, accepting the tea from Harrison.

"But, you didn't call, I had no warning," Blake replied, his eyes wide.

"Warning?" Stephanie said, looking at Blake over her glasses. "I'm your mother, not a landslip."

"I know."

"And anyway," Stephanie said, taking a sip of her tea. "We haven't seen you since you moved here. How long has it been now?"

"Almost a year," Blake replied, looking down at the floor like a child being scolded.

"And we've not heard a peep out of you," Stephanie continued. "What happened with you and Nathan in the end? Do you even speak?"

Blake and Harrison exchanged looks. The last time Blake had seen Nathan, he had ended up proving that his new partner, Davina, was heavily involved in a murder.

"It's been a while," Blake said shiftily. "I've moved on now, Mum." He put his arm around Harrison, who could not help but feel a slight air of cautiousness about him. "I'm with Harrison now."

Stephanie glanced at Harrison over her glasses as she sipped her tea. "Yes, I rather thought you might be. And how long has this been going on?"

"About six months," Harrison replied.

Stephanie nodded, then turned her head to Blake again. "Well, as it happens, we saw Nathan not so long ago."

Blake's eyes narrowed. "Did you?"

"Yes. The poor boy is miserable."

Blake raised a disdainful eyebrow. "He told you that, did he?"

"Not in so many words, no. But a mother can tell."

"You're *my* mother, not his."

Stephanie apparently chose to ignore Blake's sarcasm. "Blake, I really think you should get in touch with him."

Blake groaned and put his head in his hands. "Mum, I'm not with Nathan any more. In case you've forgotten, he cheated on me. That's why I moved to Harmschapel. And that, is why I am now in a much happier relationship with Harrison. What he is doing with his life is absolutely no concern of mine."

Again, Stephanie glanced at Harrison. "And what do *you* do?"

Blake rolled his eyes and looked at his father imploringly. "Dad, can you tell her?"

"I am entitled to ask what sort of relationship my

son is getting himself into," Stephanie replied caustically. "After all, seeing as I'm destined to be the only member of the WI without the privilege of grandchildren, I should be allowed some access into your life."

"I work in the corner shop," Harrison said, grateful for the fact that Blake was looking at Stephanie in such despair and mortification.

"A corner shop?" Stephanie repeated, looking horrified over the rim of her cup of tea.

"Yes," Harrison continued, sensing where this conversation was heading. "And I've also put my old cottage on sale, so when I've sold it, I'll have a lot of savings."

Stephanie seemed temporarily placated, but then she turned back to Blake. "Nathan was an interior designer."

"Yes, Mother, I'm aware of that," sighed Blake. "But he was also a liar and a cheater. So, let's draw a line under that, shall we? I'm with Harrison now, and nothing is going to change that."

"Stephanie, love," Colin interjected. "Will you leave the poor lad alone?"

Stephanie stiffened, but said nothing. There were a few moments of awkward silence.

"So," Blake said at last. "How long were you planning on staying for?"

"Just a few days," Stephanie said. "If you can bare

to put your mother up that is."

"And where am I supposed to sleep?" Colin grumbled. "In the car?"

Blake sighed. "I haven't got a spare room, but I guess you can have our bed. I'm up early in the morning so we'll sleep on the sofa bed. That alright with you, Harrison?"

Harrison nodded, but then his mouth fell open. He had forgotten to close the back door when he had gone out to see to Betty and she was now in the house and had managed to get, unseen, to the bags that Colin had dumped by the door. Stephanie let out a shriek of horror as the goat took a sizable chunk out of the bottom bag.

"*Argh!* How did that *thing* get in here? It's *eating* my bag! *Stop it*, Colin!"

"What am I supposed to do? What do I know about goats?" Colin exclaimed.

Harrison rushed forwards and pulled Betty away from the bags. She bleated loudly as he led her towards the still open back door and put her outside.

"Oh, it's *ruined*!" Stephanie cried, examining the corner of the bag. "This bag cost me over seventy pounds! How on Earth did a goat get in here?"

Harrison looked at the floor as he closed the back door. "She's mine, I'm sorry. She's called Betty. I thought the door was closed!"

He smiled at her, but he couldn't help but notice

Blake sighing and rubbing his eyes in exasperation.

***

That night, Blake switched off the living room light and climbed into the sofa bed beside Harrison. The evening had not especially improved. The incident with Betty had apparently done nothing to appeal Harrison to Stephanie, and she had spent the rest of the evening remaining icy and only giving short answers to anything that he had ventured to ask her. Colin on the other hand had been friendlier, and had even come out with Harrison and petted Betty whilst he fed her, but Harrison was still concerned.

Blake groaned as his head hit the pillow. "What a *day.*"

Harrison looked at him. "I know. Sorry about your mum's bag."

Blake chuckled. "Forget about it. Serves the interfering old bat right for the way she spoke to you."

"Blake, you can't call her that, she's your mum."

"You want to try growing up with her," Blake snorted. He sighed and shook his head as he stared up at the living room ceiling. "I can't believe they've just turned up out the blue like this. I don't know what I'm supposed to do with them. I'm really busy at work at the minute. Angel is working us all into the ground. He's got me in early tomorrow for a meeting."

Harrison nodded and turned onto his side. "Look, don't worry about your parents. I'm barely working this week, so I can keep them entertained."

"Doing what?"

Harrison shrugged. "Your dad looks like he appreciates a good pint. And as for your mum, well, I'll think of something."

"Take her shopping," Blake yawned, stretching out. "It'll give her a chance to look down her nose at other people and not just you. Don't worry about her. The way she talks, she makes it sound like she was head over heels for Nathan from the second she clapped eyes on him. She wasn't. It took her months. I know she means well, she just goes about it the wrong way."

"By the time I'm finished with her, she'll love me more than you do. How could she not?" Harrison grinned. "Hey, by the way. Who's Bethany?"

Blake seemed to stiffen. "Why?"

"Oh, I just saw the name written on the calendar for tomorrow."

Blake nodded and scratched the back of his head. "Just a work thing. Someone I've got to see tomorrow, it's nothing important."

"Are you two planning on nattering all night?" came a sharp sounding voice from upstairs.

Blake and Harrison exchanged looks.

"Goodnight, Mother," Blake said into the

darkness.

CHAPTER
THREE

Blake walked through the streets the next morning in dire need of caffeine, nicotine, and a full body massage. The sofa bed was a lot lumpier than he had remembered and his back was aching. He had also forgotten how heavily his dad snored, so with the sound of that reverberating around the cottage, mixed in with Betty butting the back door, confused as to why Harrison was in the lounge and not paying her any attention, it had taken Blake a good few hours to finally fall asleep.

When he arrived outside the station, the first thing

he saw was a very flashy, silver sports car parked outside. It was not a car Blake had seen before, and Harmschapel was the sort of place where a car like that stuck out like a sore thumb. Frowning, he strolled into the station.

"Morning, Sir," Darnwood said from the front desk. "You look tired."

"Thank you, Mandy," replied Blake dryly. "Whose is the car outside?"

"You'll find out," Darnwood replied, rolling her eyes. "In the meeting room. Good luck."

Blake frowned, then walked down the corridor to the meeting room. When he opened the door, he found Mattison, Patil and Gardiner waiting for him.

"You alright, Sir?" Mattison said as Blake nodded in greeting to them as he entered. "You look exhausted."

"I'm fine, Matti," Blake replied hotly. "Just didn't get much sleep. Do you know who owns the car, -"

But before he could finish his sentence, Angel's office door opened and a man that Blake had never seen before stepped out. He was wearing a beige mac and had a mass of black curls on top of his head. He was quite good looking, but Blake could immediately detect an air of arrogance about him.

"Good morning!" he said brightly. He had a distinct American accent and as he strolled towards the front of the room, he threw a wink at Patil, who broke into a shy smile, much to Mattison's obvious annoyance.

Angel followed the newcomer out of the office. "Ah, DS Harte," he said. "I'd like you to meet Detective Alec Woolf. I worked with him once, a few years ago. I got in touch to ask if he would assist us with the Pennines. Happily, he was available."

Blake stared at Woolf in disbelief. "I'm sorry?"

Woolf grinned broadly and slapped Blake on the shoulder. "Good to meet you, Harte, I've heard a lot about you. Quite the mind you've got in that head of yours."

"Detective Woolf is an accomplished detective," Angel continued. "I thought the station could do to learn a few things from him. No harm in sharpening up my officers, I'm sure you'll agree, DS Harte?"

"All the same," Woolf said, his hand still firmly gripped on Blake's shoulder. "I've not had the pleasure of being involved in some of the cases *you* have, Harte. A guy walking across water? Shot man in a shed? Genius. Mind you, I'm pretty sure I would have solved them if I'd have been there. Not to toot my own horn, but I've had my fair share of so called '*impossible crimes*.' I once was faced with a woman who had been stabbed in her bedroom, door was locked, and nobody could have gotten in or out. They brought me in because all the constables were completely stumped by it!" He laughed heartily. "Do you know how they did it?"

He looked at Blake expectantly. Then he glanced to the other officers. "How about you, honey? Any idea?" Patil glanced at Mattison who was glaring at Woolf with an expression of pure contempt, then shook her head. "What about old distinguished over here?" Woolf boomed, turning to Gardiner, who had the look of someone daring him to try and grasp his shoulder in the same way. When nobody answered, Woolf laughed loudly again. "She'd been stabbed downstairs by her husband, had stumbled upstairs and into her bedroom, locking the door behind her. Simple. God only knows why they couldn't have solved it. It just takes a bit of logical thinking. But I'm preaching to the choir there, huh?"

Blake was at a loss for words. This man was a lot to come to terms with this early in the morning.

"So," Angel said. "Let's get started, shall we? I've brought Detective Woolf up to date with the Pennines. I think we should start putting together a plan of action so that we can bring these people to justice."

Blake nodded. "Right. Okay, everyone, we, -"

"Excuse me, DS Harte," Angel interrupted. "But I was rather thinking Detective Woolf should take the meeting. He does have rather more experience with this sort of thing?"

Blake stared at Angel, swallowing down a barrage

of retorts. "You do realise I worked in Manchester before I came here, Sir? I've had plenty of experience with '*this sort of thing*.'"

"All the same," Angel said. "Detective Woolf?"

Blake paused, complete fury and disbelief coursing through him, before silently passing Woolf the marker pen he had picked up to use for the white board, and then leant against a desk with his arms folded, fully aware of the smirk coming from Gardiner behind him.

"Okay then, guys!" Woolf exclaimed loudly. He pulled the board down, the case notes and pictures that Blake had placed up from previous meetings disappearing in favour of the other side that was clear. "I thought it would be helpful to start from what we know about these scumbags then work out from there, okay? So!" He began scribbling the two names on the board. "Keith and James Pennine. A father and son, living in Clackton, which I believe is just a few miles away from this charming little village. Over the past few months, after some correspondence with other divisions, you became aware of the fact that these two were dealing in the surrounding areas. Right so far?"

"Yes," Blake said coldly. "They are wanted in connection with supplying class A's."

"Right," Woolf said. "Coke, heroin, that sort of thing."

Blake nodded.

"A raid was conducted on their property," Angel

added. "But we found no evidence. However, we do have CCTV of their activities as well as witness statements."

"So, we got our guys, but no goods. I gotcha," Woolf said, nodding.

"Every time we get close to apprehending them, they always seem to be one step ahead," Gardiner said. "Something always seems to get in our way."

"Like a tractor?" Blake muttered.

"So, we know where they live, we know what they're up to, but no solid evidence, other than CCTV of them dealing?"

"Correct," Blake said, crossing his arms. "So, what would you suggest, with all your experience?"

"These sorts of people are clever, Harte," Woolf said. "They always keep their ear to the ground, they'll be watching you as much as you're watching them. More in fact, if they can. Your goof yesterday is because they'll have been expecting you."

Again, Blake resisted the urge to release an angry reply. "So?"

"So," Woolf said, thoughtfully tapping his chin with the marker pen. "We take 'em by surprise. We wait for them. We follow 'em around if we have to. Then, when they're least expecting it, we pounce."

Blake could not hold his tongue any longer. He turned his head to Angel. "'Pounce when they're least expecting it?' You thought you needed to bring in an expert to tell me to take two suspects by surprise?"

Angel gave Blake a curt smile. "Would you say, DS Harte, given the run of events thus far, that you have managed to take either Keith or James Pennine by surprise?"

"Well, obviously we haven't, -"

"So, that being the case, in what way is Detective Woolf giving you unhelpful advice?"

"Harte, don't worry about it," Woolf said, slapping Blake on the shoulder again. Blake was now quite close to taking the board marker out of Woolf's hand and thrusting it up his nose. "I'd be the same in your position. Young, good looking upstart like me coming along and calling the shots, I get it. But, be honest. Your way isn't working so far. Stick with me, don't be afraid to learn off someone else. I've already cleared it with the boss. Today, me and you are going out there and we're gonna bring these scumbags in and nail them. It might take us all day, but we will find them. I've already got some correspondence with another station with word of where they are. Trust me, Harte! We've got this. You seen my wheels outside?"

"I did."

"My pride and joy. The Mazda Miata. She's a couple of decades old, but that car has never let me down. Plus, it's unmarked, so we can get nice and close to the Pennines without them noticing us."

"You think," Blake said, moving himself away

from Woolf before he could place his hands on him again. "That we can be inconspicuous in a silver sports car?"

"Trust me," Woolf said again.

Blake had never trusted anybody less in his entire life.

CHAPTER
FOUR

Harrison stepped out the shower, the ache in his back from a rogue spring in the sofa bed having slowly diminished. It was still much earlier than he was used to being awake on a day off but, as he had expected, Stephanie and Colin were up very soon after Blake had left for work, and while he could certainly picture Colin joining him in vegetating in front of the television for the day, he suspected that Stephanie would require slightly more in the way of entertainment.

Blake's parents were now downstairs eating

breakfast so he was free to go into the bedroom and get changed. He was just pulling a shirt over his head when he heard Stephanie mention his name from downstairs. Finding he could not resist the urge to listen to what she was saying, he crept across the bedroom and gently pulled the door open, listening to the conversation downstairs. It sounded like Colin was defending him.

"-perfectly nice lad, Stephanie, come on, love."

"Did I say otherwise?" Stephanie said loftily. Though he had only known her for less than a day, Harrison could picture her looking over her glasses at her husband. "I just don't think that he's *right* for Blake."

"He's given you *no* reason to think that though, love!" Colin replied. "You've known him less than twenty four hours."

"Colin, I have always been a better reader of situations than you. Think about it. He works in a corner shop. Blake is a detective sergeant in a busy police station. It is hardly an equal footing."

"What's *that* got to do with anything?" Colin asked incredulously. Harrison could feel his respect for Blake's father growing by the second.

"Harrison is a young man, younger than Blake by quite a few years. He takes after you, I expect. Young piece of skirt and his crotch does the rest."

"I'd hardly call Harrison a young piece of skirt,

you daft bat."

"It's about *money,*" Stephanie pressed on, lowering her voice. "I don't blame Harrison as such, and I'm sure that there is some genuine affection there, but we're the next generation, Colin, we're supposed to be the ones thinking practically. He's young, he'll be wanting to set himself up for the future. Blake's wage would do that!"

"Were you not listening last night woman? He's fine for money. He's got savings, more than I did at his age, more than *you* did. You're just upset he's not Nathan."

"Oh, don't be ridiculous, Colin," Stephanie snapped.

"No, you loved Nathan. You haven't listened to a word Blake's said about that, and anyway, it's none of our *business!*"

Harrison heard Stephanie tut loudly. "That is so *typical* of you," she hissed. "He's our *son.* Of course it's our business. So his relationship hit a bit of rough patch, it's our jobs as parents to show him that relationships need care and work. It's not always easy."

"You're telling me," Colin muttered.

Harrison had to stifle a laugh. He could only imagine what being married to Stephanie must be like. He rather thought Colin deserved a medal. But his smile quickly faded when he heard what she said next.

"Blake will be thinking it too. Mark my words. I

know he's still thinking about Nathan, I saw it in his face when that damn goat was in here. Embarrassment! Shame! Nathan would *never* have done something like that. Why do you think he hasn't told us about Harrison in the first place? Because, deep down he knows that he ran out on Nathan too quickly. I know my son. Better than he knows himself, I'd wager. This is *not* a relationship that is going to last."

Harrison leant his head against the door, his head whirring. As hard as it had been to listen to Stephanie's assessment of him and the relationship, she was absolutely right. Why had Blake never mentioned him to his parents? Since they had officially been together, Blake had shown nothing but disdain for his ex and the reasons they broke up, and Harrison's self-confidence had grown as a result, but now he could feel his mind flirting with those old feelings again, as Stephanie's words repeated in his head.

Soon, he heard her complaining about how long he was taking in the shower and so, though it was the last thing he wanted to do, he strolled downstairs with a forced smile.

"Sorry to keep you waiting," he said in a tone he hoped was cheerful. "Shall we go?"

***

To Harrison's surprise, Stephanie seemed rather enchanted with Harmschapel.

SPOTLIGHT

"It really is a lovely place," she said fondly as they wandered through the village. "So picturesque. It's like something you'd see in a classical painting."

Harrison gave her a brief smile. "Yeah, I suppose it is. You kind of get used to it when you've lived here all your life."

The sound of wheezing behind him alerted Harrison to the fact that Colin was clearly struggling with the hill they were climbing. "Are you alright?" Harrison asked him, slowing down.

"Aye, aye," panted Colin. "I'll be fine, lad. Just takes me a little bit longer to do these treks these days. Not her, mind." He nodded his head at Stephanie who was striding far in front of them. "She could climb Everest. Hey, listen, son," he murmured, pulling Harrison closer. "Has it got a pub, this village? Only, I could do with a drink. It's thirsty work climbing this hill."

Harrison nodded. "We've got The Dog's Tail. It's a nice place, I think you'll like it. It's just at the bottom of this hill."

Colin nodded gratefully as they reached the top and began the journey down, his speed noticeably picking up at the thought of what the pub had to offer him. Harrison liked him, he reminded him of a Grandfather he had had when he was little. Granddad Joe had died when Harrison was very small, but he had vague memories of a warm, earthy man sneaking him sweets with a wink underneath the table while his mother was cooking the dinner. Harrison hoped that how well he was getting on with Colin would be helpful in changing Stephanie's way of thinking that he was not right for Blake.

When they got to The Dog's Tail, Colin walked towards the bar and ordered them all drinks, pints for him and Harrison and a small sherry for Stephanie. While they waited, Harrison and Stephanie sat in silence for a few moments until Harrison turned to her.

"So, you like Harmschapel then?"

Stephanie nodded thoughtfully. "Yes. I could see me being quite happy in a place like this."

"Oh, are you thinking of moving?"

Stephanie pursed her lips as Colin brought the drinks over on a tray. "We're getting quite close to retirement age. We must think of the future. But I think a village environment would suit me quite well. And the country air would do wonders for Colin, wouldn't it?"

"Yes, dear," Colin said automatically, taking a sizable swig of his pint.

"Where are *your* parents, by the way?" Stephanie asked. "Do they live 'round here?"

Harrison froze, his pint a few inches from his lips. "Erm, no, they live away, actually."

"Away?" Stephanie pressed, looking at him over

her glasses.

Harrison was starting to think that that look was the only reason she owned glasses. His mind raced. He was not sure that the time was right to inform Stephanie that both of his parents were in prison for the murder of his ex-boyfriend.

He was saved from having to think of a story when the pub door opened and Jacqueline, Blake's landlady, walked in. She was wearing a short skirt that, in typical Jacqueline fashion, was too young for her, and her faded red hair was up in her usual, heavily hair sprayed, beehive. She smiled warmly when she saw Harrison.

"Hello, Harrison! Lovely to see you. And who's this?"

She looked down at Colin and beamed at him, with a slight flutter of her eyelashes. "Jacqueline. I'm Harrison's landlady. I live just across the road from him in the cottage opposite."

Colin glanced at Stephanie who was taking in Jacqueline's outfit with a distinct air of distaste. "Oh, aye. I'm Colin, this is my wife, Stephanie."

"A pleasure," Stephanie said, somewhat sharply.

"We're Blake's parents," Colin added.

"Oh, *see!*" Jacqueline said, clapping her hands together. "Oh, but this must be the first time you've seen him since he moved to Harmschapel. Where is he?"

"He's at work," Harrison replied.

"And it falls to *you* to entertain the in-laws," Jacqueline chuckled, nodding at Harrison. "I see how it is. Well, welcome to Harmschapel, I'm sure I'll see you around." She threw another flirtatious look in Colin's direction and then tottered off towards the bar.

Stephanie stared at her as Jacqueline hauled herself on to a barstool, and threw one leg over the other. "Is she a prostitute?" she asked Harrison, her eyes wide.

All Harrison could do was shake his head.

Eventually, he excused himself from the table and walked into the toilets, locking himself in one of the cubicles so that he could ring Blake. As the ringing tone buzzed in his ear, he prayed inwardly that Blake was going to get out of work on time. Harrison was unsure how much longer he could spend trying to keep Stephanie happy and he was starting to feel extremely stressed.

When Blake answered, he sounded tired and extremely irritable. "Hello?"

"Hey, it's me," Harrison said, sitting down on the seat of the toilet. "How's it going?"

"Not great," Blake replied shortly. "What's up?"

"I was just wondering what time you're going to be back tonight. I'm kind of running out of things to show your parents for the day."

"I don't *know* yet Harrison," Blake snapped. Harrison recoiled slightly at his tone. "Right now, I'm in the middle of watching someone, so this really isn't a good time to check up on me, alright?"

Harrison felt a twinge of anger, unsure of what to say now. He had wanted to confide in Blake as to what he had heard Stephanie saying that morning, but he was apparently not in the mood.

"Alright, *fine,*" Harrison snapped back. "And if you're quite finished chewing on my head, I'll have it back, please. I need to go and entertain *your* parents for the rest of the night." He heard Blake start to reply, but before he could stop himself, Harrison had hung up. For a few seconds he stared at his phone. He had never spoken to Blake like that before.

"Brilliant. Well done, Harrison," he muttered bitterly to himself. On top of everything else, he and Blake had just had their first row. He took a deep breath and, pushing the white noise that was now buzzing round his head as to whose fault it had been, he left the cubicle and walked back into the bar. What greeted him did not improve things.

Stephanie was stood up, staring at him, her eyes wide. "*Prison?*" she exclaimed. "Your parents are both in *prison?*"

Harrison's mouth fell open in horror before he glanced at an extremely abashed Jacqueline who was sat on her bar stool with her head in her hands. "*Sorry,*" she mouthed. Her face was as red as her hair and she looked incredibly guilty.

Stephanie put her glasses on from round her neck and looked over them at Harrison. "I think we need to have a little talk, Harrison. Don't you?"

CHAPTER
FIVE

Blake stared at his reflection in the rear-view mirror in disbelief, his mobile still clutched in his hand. "Blake Sebastian Harte," he said under his breath, "you are an absolute *idiot.*"

Why had he snapped at Harrison like that? Blake knew more than anyone what a day in his mother's company could be like and Harrison was under no obligation to entertain his parents for the day. He sighed and put his head back on the headrest. He made a mental note to go to the shop on his way home, whenever that actually happened, and buy

Harrison a selection of apology gifts. He also felt guilty for lying to him about why the name *'Bethany'* was written on the calendar. It somehow had completely slipped his mind, and even his parents turning up had failed to jog his memory, though now he thought about it, it should have been obvious why they had.

The reason Blake was in such a foul mood was because of his current situation. After leaving the station with Woolf, who Blake was finding more and more irritating as the hours drew on, they had driven in his silver sports car to a small, rundown carpark that had only ever vaguely brushed against Blake's peripheral whenever he had driven past it on a drive in the direction of Clackton, a large town a few miles away from Harmschapel. A few hundred yards away was a decrepit petrol station that was still running, but which Blake had never thought to enter. It was this petrol station that Woolf had decided was worth them sitting here until they saw their targets.

Blake glanced up at the rear-view mirror again. Woolf was making his way back to the car having gone into a clump of bushes to relieve himself.

"Sorry about that, Harte," Woolf said cheerily, climbing back into the driver's seat. "When you gotta go, you gotta go."

Blake shook his head. "We've been sat here for hours, what exactly are you hoping to see?"

"Patience, Harte," Woolf replied soothingly. "I

told you, I have it on good authority that James Pennine, the son, works at that gas station. I also happen to know that when he is working, his father always comes to pick him up at the end of his shift. All we have to do is wait. Then, we act."

"Then if the son is in there, why don't we just go and bring him in?"

"Cause we want the full package," Woolf said slowly. "The dad and the kid." He pulled a packet of cigarettes out of his pocket and offered it to Blake. "You smoke?"

Blake stared desperately at the packet. He had been trying to give up smoking for the best part of a year but kept failing.

"You mind if I do?" Without waiting for an answer, Woolf lit the cigarette with a clipper lighter and flamboyantly snapped the lid back down with a *'snap.'* The smoke instantly wafted towards Blake, setting his cravings on edge.

"So, where did Angel find you?" Blake asked, in an effort to distract himself.

"London," Woolf replied, checking his hair in the driver's mirror. "I met him while we were working on a case similar to this. Much bigger, of course."

"Of course," replied Blake sardonically.

"I mean, we're talking wide scale. I cracked that case right through the middle, impressed him, he kept my details. I'm kind of free agent, ya see, Harte. I go where I'm needed. Of course, back home, things were a lot easier. Such a weird country you've got here. We're armed over there, so I don't get anywhere near as much crap from suspects as I do here."

"Just wave a gun, and everything solves itself, right?" Blake said.

"You got it. I know you guys are all scared of guns over here, but it gets results."

"Yeah, it also causes the problems you need to get results for," Blake replied. "But I don't think this is the time for that conversation. You're right. It's different over here."

Woolf merely shrugged and took a long pull on his cigarette. "So, that chick who works at the station."

Blake rolled his eyes. "You mean Mini?"

"Mini," repeated Woolf, smiling. Blake had to admit his teeth were shining white. "She single?"

"No. She's in a very happy relationship with Matti. That's the younger officer."

"Happy relationship, huh?" Woolf grinned. "I've heard that one before."

Blake shook his head in disbelief but said nothing.

For the next few hours, Blake remained as quiet as he could manage. Woolf continued bragging about all the huge cases he had solved single handily to the point that Blake doubted that Woolf would even notice if he got out and went home, which as time went on, was a prospect that was becoming more and more tempting.

The sun began to set on the horizon, and soon they were sat in darkness.

Woolf had just begun to tell Blake how it would be impossible to find anybody who knew more about cars than he did when there was movement from the entrance to the petrol station. A young man who Blake recognised as James Pennine stepped out and wandered along the forecourt. He was wearing a black polo neck, which Blake assumed was the uniform for the petrol station, and was looking up the road.

"...Course, this baby I got cheap. If you find yourself faced with a dealer who doesn't know what they're talking about, it's too easy to get yourself the best deal -"

"Shut up," Blake said suddenly. "Look, he's there."

Woolf narrowed his eyes and stared at James. "See, Harte? What did I tell you? Look at him, he's waiting for his dad."

Sure enough, two headlights appeared in the distance and as it got closer, Blake recognised the car as the one he had been pursuing with Gardiner the day before.

"Okay," Woolf said sharply. "Let's go."

Trying not to let Woolf ordering him about get on his last nerve, Blake opened the car door and began walking towards the petrol station, with Woolf a few steps behind. They crossed the road, still unnoticed by

James as the car pulled up next to him. When they were only a few feet away, Blake pulled out his identification. "James Pennine?"

James looked up at Blake as he opened the passenger door of the car, his mouth falling open. As they reached the car, Woolf leaned down to knock on the driver's window. The rough, angry face of Keith Pennine glared back at them.

"Would you both like to come with us?" Woolf said, producing his own ID. "We'd like to have a little chat with you both."

There was a pause, then Keith turned to his son and yelled "*Get in!*"

At once, James leapt into the car. Before he had even closed the door, the car's wheels screeched loudly as Keith began reversing.

"*Harte!*" shouted Woolf. Blake turned in surprise to see Woolf already halfway back to the car. "*Hurry up!*"

Blake let out a groan of frustration as the Pennines rapidly reversed and swung the car around in the middle of the forecourt. He ran across the road and jumped in the passenger seat. He stared expectantly at Woolf out of the windscreen as he leant across the bonnet of the car and grinned excitedly at Blake. "Now you're gonna see how we do these chases in the States."

Blake widened his eyes in disbelief. "Will you just get in? They're getting away!"

Woolf tapped the bonnet again with both hands and then climbed into the driver's seat, starting the car. As he did, Blake heard a loud rumble. He thought it was the engine of the car, but then heavy rain immediately hammered down around them. Woolf slammed his foot down and spun the steering wheel aggressively. The car immediately swung around, rocketing off in the direction of the Pennines.

At first, they seemed quite far ahead, but it did not take long for Woolf to catch up. As the rain battered the windscreen, Woolf let out a harsh laugh. "Oh, *this* is what I'm talking about!"

Blake merely shook his head incredulously.

As the chase continued, the rain only seemed to get heavier. The evening light seemed to have quickly vanished, and soon it was so dark that the only time Blake could fully see out of the windscreen was when the wipers cleared the rain from the glass, though it quickly was replaced. The Pennines' car was less flashy than the sports car, but that did not seem to stop them from tearing along the road. Before too long, Blake just could make out the silhouette of St Abra's church in the middle of Harmschapel, which meant that they were now speeding through the village.

"They're going to kill someone at this rate," Blake said, as the vague shapes of buildings whizzed past them in the dark. "Or we are. You're going to have to slow down."

"No can do, Harte," Woolf replied, grabbing the gearstick and ramming it forwards. "Lesson one of a car chase, if the suspect is driving crazy, you have to as well. Don't worry, I've done this hundreds of times. They're not getting away this time."

By more luck than judgement, in Blake's opinion, the lights around them vanished, meaning they had managed to clear the village without serious incident, but Blake was now all too aware of the winding country roads coming up ahead of them, and the rain seemed to somehow be getting heavier.

"The roads are curved 'round here, be careful!" Blake cried. Woolf said nothing. His eyes were fixed on the road ahead of them. The rear lights of the Pennines' car were still visible ahead of them, but the corners were now coming faster than Blake was comfortable with.

The car ahead skidded around the first one and Woolf did the same, causing Blake to grab the side of his seat. Blake had to admit that Woolf was driving with incredible skill, certainly more than the Pennines as soon the rear of their car was getting closer. By the time they had slewed around the third sharp bend, the Pennines were inches in front of them. In the distance, from the headlights from Woolf's car, Blake could make out the passing point in the road telling them that Clifton Moore tunnel was just ahead. Blake had just begun inwardly praying that the road through the tunnel was clear, when Woolf cursed loudly. The Pennines car was slowing down, but aggressively, not out of caution.

"What the hell is he *doing?* He's trying to ram us!" Woolf bellowed, attempting to brake, but it was too late. The car slammed into the back of the Pennines with a loud crunch. Though neither car stopped moving, they were immediately plunged into complete darkness. Blake felt the car slow down further.

"They've smashed my headlights," Woolf cried. "Oh, they are going to *pay* for that."

"What are you *doing?*" Blake shouted urgently. "We can't go on at this speed with no headlights in this weather!"

"They've got no lights either," Woolf said, seemingly ignoring Blake. He was right. For a few moments, the collision looked like it had also smashed the rear lights of the Pennines' car. But then, as they entered the tunnel, they saw the red lights of the back of the car appear in front of them again.

"We've got them now!" Woolf announced triumphantly. The tight curve in the tunnel brought the bricks around them closer than Blake could handle, and he gritted his teeth in preparation for the crash. Then, the red lights in front of them disappeared again, the bulbs apparently giving up completely. A second later, Woolf's headlights came on again, illuminating the road in front of them.

"We've got them – *what the…?*"

Blake frowned and stared through the windscreen with his mouth open wide. They came out of the tunnel and Woolf hit the brakes, bringing them at last to a stop. But they were alone.

As soon as the car had stopped, Blake got out and stared around them in disbelief. The Pennines' vehicle was nowhere to be seen. As the rain continued hammering around them, soaking Blake almost immediately, he turned around to face the tunnel again, the incomprehension of the situation rendering him speechless. Somehow, the Pennines' car had completely vanished while they had been speeding through the narrow, dark tunnel.

CHAPTER
SIX

It did not take long for the other officers from Harmschapel police station to make their way to the scene. The rain had finally died down, and Woolf had moved his car to a passing spot close to the exit of the tunnel. Blake was sat by the side of the road, silently, desperately trying to work out how what he had just witnessed had happened. The Pennines had been just in front of them, he had seen the rear lights of their car clearly. Then, in a second, in the time it had taken for those lights to go off again and Woolf's to come back on, they had completely disappeared. It was impossible.

Mattison walked towards Blake and broke into his thoughts. "We've closed the road, Sir. Nothing can come from either direction."

Blake nodded. "Did you get the torch?"

Mattison handed it over, giving Blake a tentative look. "Are you sure about this, Sir? I mean, a car can't just vanish. Nothing can."

Blake did not reply. Instead, he grasped hold of the torch and strolled into the tunnel, shining the light around the walls as he followed the road. Around him, the tunnel was cramped, bricked up, and murky, but, as he had expected, absolutely solid. There was nothing to suggest that any tampering of any kind had gone on to make what he had seen happen. He slowly walked along the tunnel until he arrived at the entrance, where Woolf had driven them in. When he arrived at the opening, he found Angel waiting for him, his arms crossed and a stern expression on his face.

"Rather farfetched, DS Harte," he said levelly. Blake just nodded. It was certainly one way to describe it. "I understand from Detective Woolf that you were in pursuit of both suspects? Keith Pennine and his son?"

"That's right," murmured Blake.

"I'm telling you, boss," Woolf added, appearing behind Blake. "They were both in that car. We saw them before we started chasing them. And before we even went in that tunnel, we rammed into the back of them! I don't get it."

Blake looked down at the road. Just visible on the wet tarmac were the tyre tracks where Woolf had skidded his car around the bend in the tunnel, the same bend where the Pennines' car seemed to have just disintegrated into thin air. Despite everything, he was finding it difficult to not be slightly pleased that Woolf seemed as dumbfounded by it all as he was.

"I think it's quite obvious that you have both been the victim of an elaborate hoax," Angel said as he closed the notebook he had been writing in. "Needless to say, I shall be wanting to speak to you both tomorrow morning. I trust I will be able to leave you to finish off here?"

Blake nodded as he watched Angel walk back to his car, calmly climb in, and drive off in the direction of Harmschapel.

"Don't feel down, Sir," Mattison murmured as they watched Angel's car disappear. "If everything happened the way you said it did, I'd like to see him manage to work it out."

Despite his foul mood, Blake smiled. "Thanks, Matti. So, do we have anything? Anything at all that can point towards how they did this?"

"We've checked the masonry, Sir," Patil called, her voice echoing around the tunnel. "It's like you said.

It's all solid brick. Nothing's been moved, there's no way they could have got out of here without going through the other end. The tunnel's too narrow for you to have even overtaken them without realising." She walked outside and shook her head, baffled. "I know we've had some weird cases before, Sir, but this one tops it.

Blake sighed and scratched the back of his head. He did not have the slightest clue on where to begin trying to piece it together.

"Still though," Woolf said gruffly as he lit another cigarette, his fourth since the rest of the team had arrived. "This changes nothing. They can't have gone that far."

"What do you think they're doing? Hiding in the ceiling?" Blake snapped. "They've completely taken us for a ride, and you know it."

"Harte, chill out, man," Woolf replied calmly. "I know, it's weird. But there isn't a criminal walking that can keep me fooled for long. They've won this round, I'll give 'em that. But we *will* find them. Trust me."

***

By the time Blake finally arrived home, it was close to midnight. The evening had been spent fruitlessly trying to find a single scrap of evidence that could point them in the right direction, but they had found nothing. In the end, Blake had told the team to reopen the road, and sent everyone home, in the vein hope that things would become clearer after a good night's sleep. He felt exhausted, but he knew that it would take hours for him to fall asleep. His head was buzzing too loudly with the incomprehensibility of the day's events. When he walked into the house, he found Harrison sitting alone in the living room.

"Hi," he said wearily. "I cannot begin to tell you the day I have had."

Harrison barely looked up from the television. "Yeah. I could say the same to you."

For a moment, Blake was confused by Harrison's cold tone, but then he remembered their earlier phone conversation. He sighed and walked towards Harrison, wrapping his arms around his shoulders. "Look, I am *so* sorry about biting your head off. I was the one in the wrong, I had no right snapping at you like that. It won't happen again, I promise."

Harrison stood up, shook Blake's hands off him, and strolled into the kitchen. "I've heard that before, Blake."

It took Blake a couple of seconds to land on what Harrison was getting at, but when he realised, his mouth fell open in outrage. "Are you *serious*?"

Harrison leant against the kitchen counter, his hands on his head. Blake could tell he immediately regretted his words, but they stung nevertheless. He folded his arms and looked at him seriously. "Harrison, you can't compare me snarling at you 'cause of the day I've had, compared to…" His voice trailed off, he was sure he did not need to explicitly mention Harrison's abusive ex-boyfriend. Harrison looked down at the floor and said nothing. "What's brought this on?"

"Your mum," Harrison replied quietly.

Blake groaned and looked up at the ceiling. "Oh, what has she said?"

Harrison looked up at him, more annoyed than Blake had ever seen him. "It's not so much what *she* said, Blake, it's more what *you didn't* say."

"What do you mean?"

"We ran into Jacqueline at The Dog's Tail," Harrison replied sharply. "While I was on the phone to you, Stephanie managed to get out of her everything that had happened with Mum and Dad, as well as my history with Daniel. It took her about two minutes to find out that the guy her son is now with let all those things happen to him. As far as she's concerned, I'm just about the worst thing that could possibly have happened to you."

Blake stared at him in disbelief. "How can she think that?"

"Because you didn't *tell* her about me, Blake! She sees me as some mucky little secret you wanted to keep hidden. And do you know what the worst bit is? I couldn't argue with her. Because I don't *know* why you didn't tell them! Unless you are that ashamed of me?"

Blake put his head in his hands. "Of course I'm not, Harrison."

"Do you know what she said to me? '*Both parents in prison for murder? How do we know that the apple doesn't fall far from the tree?*' She actually *thinks* that I could be capable of something like that, Blake. And all because you didn't tell her that you were in a new relationship. Why didn't you say anything?"

Blake sighed and held his hands out. "*This* is why, Harrison. Because she can't help poking her nose in. She doesn't mean to come across as such a battle axe, it's just her way."

Harrison shook his head. "That doesn't answer my question, Blake, and you know it. She was going to find out at some point. If it wasn't for your dad, I dunno how I would have even handled today. She treated me like I was some sort of intruder! Then when she found out about my parents, she basically told me that I was bad news for you. I even heard her say to your dad – '*Nathan would never have caused us this sort of worry.*'"

Blake could see that Harrison was starting to get quite worked up, so he walked towards him and placed his arms around him. "Look, *stop*. Okay? Just stop."

"I *can't*, Blake!" Harrison cried, again, shaking

himself free. "She made me feel about *that* big."

"Who cares what my mum thinks though? This is just what she gets like!" Blake argued back. "I told you, she treated Nathan exactly the same when she first met him!"

Harrison sighed and walked towards the stairs. "It's all well and good you saying *'who cares,'* Blake. But you seem to be forgetting that you are the reason that I'm even here in the first place. You came into my life, and suddenly everything changes. I hadn't even known you a week before both my parents ended up in prison, leaving me alone with only a *goat* for a friend. I'm trying to rebuild my life, and I'm sorry, but you're pretty much the main part of that, because I haven't got anything or anyone else. And when I've got your family wanting me gone because you didn't think to mention me, I'm sorry, but I *do* care." He turned and walked up the stairs.

Blake did not know what to say. Throughout their relationship up to this point, he had tried his hardest to try and relieve Harrison of some of the anxiety he had had to live with, and as proud as he was that he felt that he could say things like that to him, it still was not easy to hear. "Where are you going?"

"I'm going to bed."

"Where are my parents?"

"Oh," Harrison said bitterly, turning on the stairs. "They went to the B&B. I don't think your mum wanted to share a house with me. You know, with me being such a *terrible* person."

And with that, he climbed the stairs, leaving Blake alone in the dark kitchen, his only company being his own thoughts after what had been a pretty awful day.

ROBERT INNES

CHAPTER
SEVEN

Another night of broken sleep resulted in Blake feeling exhausted when the alarm went off the next morning. As soon as he opened his eyes, the previous night's argument landed loudly in his head. Blake glanced across at Harrison, who was lying on his side, his back to him. His usual soft snores were missing, leading Blake to the conclusion that Harrison was pretending to be asleep. He briefly toyed with the idea of checking, but decided against it. He was tired and his brain wasn't clear enough at this moment to try and reason with a clearly still upset Harrison.

Instead, he picked up his uniform from the chair and took them into the bathroom with him, changing straight into them after his shower. He then went downstairs and made himself a pot of tea while he tried to put together the broken jigsaw puzzle that resembled his brain that morning. It was bad enough that he had argued with Harrison, but the bizarre events with the Pennines' car only added to his problems. He had hoped that a night's sleep would trigger something in his brain to give him a clue as to how the impossible feat had been accomplished, but if anything, he was more confused now than he had been when he had been standing at the mouth of the tunnel.

He sighed and took a long pull on his ecig, glancing out of the kitchen window. Just visible through the trees on the other side of the road was the B&B his parents were currently staying. He blew the vapour out of his nose like a dragon, a surge of annoyance pulsing through him as he imagined how his mother had spoken to Harrison that had resulted in him feeling so upset. He drank his tea as quickly as the temperature of it allowed, and made a mental note that he was going to speak to his father alone before the day was out. He was just searching for his house keys when he felt his mobile ringing in his pocket. He scowled at the screen, not recognising the number. It was too early even for a cold caller, so he put the phone to his ear while he hunted around for the keys. A familiar voice made him roll his eyes.

"Harte, it's Detective Woolf. Hope I didn't wake you."

Blake glanced at the clock on the wall. "So do I, considering I'm supposed to be in in twenty minutes. How did you get my number?"

"Inspector Angel," replied Woolf shortly. "There's been a development, Harte."

Blake frowned as he finally laid his hands on his keys, which had fallen down the back of the fruit bowl. "What sort of development?"

Woolf paused, presumably for dramatic effect. "We've found the car."

***

Though the fire had been put out, the smell of burning fuel still hung in the air. It was acrid and made it difficult to breath.

Blake, Mattison, Woolf and Patil were close to a field in a remote part of the countryside, a few miles away from the exit to the tunnel. The car that had somehow disappeared the night before was now a shadow of its former self, an abandoned burnt out shell, with only the bent and charred metal framework still resembling its previous shape.

"It's the car, alright," Woolf said, "But what the hell is it doing out here?"

"Who found it?" Blake asked, staring at the husk of the vehicle.

"A couple were driving towards Harmschapel this morning, Sir," Mattison replied, passing him a document. "They saw it in the distance, just as the petrol tank blew. They said it threw a massive fireball up in to the air. Here's the report from the fire services. Not that they needed to tell us, but they say it was deliberate. They found a discarded petrol tank in the bushes."

Blake skimmed through the report before looking up at the car again, with a frown. "Why?" he murmured. "First they make it vanish, then they blow it up. And I'm guessing no sign of Keith and James Pennine anywhere?"

Patil shook her head. "Nothing, Sir. They're probably miles away by now."

Blake sighed and looked around him. It seemed like they were in the middle of nowhere. It was the perfect place to dump a car, but where had the Pennines disappeared to from here? It was all making less sense by the minute.

Then, Blake spotted a house in the distance. "There," he said pointing to it. "That house. It's only about a mile away."

"Just what I was thinking," Woolf said sharply,

standing up from where he had been engrossed in the registration plate, paying no attention to the house whatsoever. "They might have seen or heard something."

"Actually," Blake replied. "I was thinking that unless the Pennines were picked up and taken somewhere else from here, then that house might be a good hideout."

Woolf scratched his chin. "Good, yeah. I was about to say the same thing. Okay, let's go." He began to walk towards the police car they had arrived in, but Blake stopped him.

"Do you know what would be *really* helpful, Detective Woolf? I need somebody to return to the station to get in touch with forensics. Sharon will have a field day with this."

Woolf narrowed his eyes. "I think I would be much more help checking out the house, Harte."

"Still, this is *my* investigation, and I would prefer a more senior officer to be back at base, inform Angel what we've found, file the fire report, things like that." Blake hated being so petty, but Woolf seemed to just bring it out of him.

Woolf bit his lip in annoyance. "Fine. Well, me and Mini can go back together then." He turned his head to Patil and winked at her. "Can't we, sweetheart?"

Patil raised a disdainful eyebrow as Mattison

folded his arms and glared at Woolf. "Actually, Sir," he said to Blake. "I'd prefer go with Detective Woolf while you and Mini go and check out the house, if that's alright with you?"

Blake smiled, hoping it looked more professional than smug. "Good idea, Matti. We've got enough officers here to wait for forensics. With me, Mini."

As Blake and Patil walked towards their car, Blake looked back and was pleased to see Woolf looking sheepish as Mattison continued glaring at him.

***

When they arrived at the house, everything seemed quiet. It looked a building that at one time had been quite opulent, but had been allowed to fall into disrepair. The lawn in the front garden was overgrown, nettles and brambles spilling out onto the road over the fence, which consisted of mostly rotting wood. Blake stared at the dusty windows for a few moments.

"Does anyone even live here?" Patil asked.

"Let's go find out," Blake replied as they got out of the car. "Keep your wits about you. The Pennines could be here."

Patil nodded as they walked slowly up the garden path. There was an overflowing wheelie bin halfway down and as they got closer, Blake felt glass crunching under his feet. He looked around the yard. It certainly looked deserted. No house proud person would surely want to live here. When they arrived at one of the windows, Blake put his face against the glass and peered in. Though the window was filthy, he could just make out a living room. It looked more like a pigsty; there were takeaway cartons, discarded beer bottles, mouldy mugs, and dusty clothes discarded around the ancient looking furniture. "Someone *has* been here," Blake murmured. "Come on."

He walked round to the front door and knocked. When he got no answer, he knelt down and lifted up the flap of the letter box, which immediately came loose from the door and clattered onto the ground. Blake peered through the slot. Inside, was more of the same. The hallway leading to what Blake could see was the kitchen was in an even worse state than the living room. Old papers, dirt, and even a large black rat scurrying around, chewing at a pile of discarded food on the floor.

"Sir!" Patil whispered urgently. Blake turned his head to where she was. She was peering through the window of what looked like an extension to the house. "There's someone in there," she said.

As Blake looked through the glass, he could just make out a figure, standing, perfectly still, though he could not make out their face, or surroundings. "Hello?" he said loudly, banging on the glass. The figure didn't move. There was a door to the side of them that lead into the room. Blake tried to turn the handle. It was locked. He knocked sharply on the door. "Hello! Can you come out please?" Still, the figure did not move, despite Blake banging on the window again.

"Shall I?" Patil said grimly, stepping back and raising her foot up. Blake sighed as he considered their options. Whoever was in there was clearly thinking they could not be seen and when they were looking for two dangerous men like the Pennines, it seemed that breaking their way in was their only choice. Blake nodded and Patil immediately began kicking the door in. After the third kick, the door burst open.

They walked into what looked like a cellar. The floor was made out of old wooden planks, and there was a repugnant smell that hit their nostrils. But when they saw what was inside, they quickly forgot the smell. The figure was hanging from the ceiling, a large bulky rope around his neck. He stared vacantly at them, his tongue lolling slightly out of his mouth, his whole body limp; he was dead.

"Oh my god," Patil murmured. "Is that…?"

"Yeah," Blake replied quietly, his mouth dry. "It's James Pennine."

CHAPTER
EIGHT

Betty looked up at Harrison intently as he closed the cottage door behind them. As much as Harrison would have liked to believe that she could sense his low mood, it was far more likely that she was just being impatient. He set off down the road with her, his chest heavy, thinking back over the argument with Blake with regret. Angry as he was that Blake had completely neglected to tell his parents about him, it had been unfair to blame him fully for Stephanie's response to what she had discovered.

As he walked through the village, taking care not to give Betty access to the villager's plants hanging over the fences, he began to mentally rehearse what he was going to say to Blake, to try and rectify things, but his mind seemed to go blank after the word *'sorry.'* And there were still, after all, things that Blake had not answered.

"Harrison?"

Harrison turned to where the voice had come from, his heart sinking slightly as he saw Colin walking towards him. "You alright, lad?"

Harrison nodded. "Yeah, not bad thanks. You out on your own?"

"Aye," replied Colin, looking relieved. "She's having a nap. It takes it out of her poking her nose in where it doesn't belong, bless her soul."

Harrison gave a small smile, feeling slightly better. Colin glanced down at Betty and frowned. "You take that goat for walks?"

"Yeah," Harrison said, pulling Betty closer to him, aware that she was staring at Mrs Featherstone's hydrangeas with a hungry look in her eyes. "She spends a fair bit of time in the back garden so I like to give her a bit of enrichment. That and I like spending time with her. Is that weird?"

Colin chuckled and smiled. "Nah. I don't think so. Mind if I come with you?"

Harrison was surprised, but nodded, and the two

of them began to walk down the road together.

"Listen, lad," Colin began, looking over his shoulder towards the B&B. "Don't think too badly of Stephanie. She's a good'un, really. She's always wrapped Blake up in cotton wool. He's her only child."

"I'm an only child too." He thought about how far his own parents had gone to '*protect him*' in their own way. Suddenly, Stephanie's methods seemed slightly more normal.

They walked a bit further in silence before Colin said, "He wasn't an only child. Not at first."

Harrison stopped and stared at Colin. "What do you mean?"

"Has Blake never told you?"

Harrison shook his head. Colin sighed as they began walking again. "Twenty years ago. Blake was ten, and his sister, Bethany, she was eight."

Harrison's insides went cold. He almost felt too scared to ask. "What happened?"

Colin stared straight ahead. "She got hit by a car. I was at work; Stephanie and the kids were out in the garden. Stephanie went inside to answer the phone while the kids were playing and, well. You know what kids are like at that age. No fears, the world is there to explore. Anyway, the only thing Stephanie heard was a car's brakes and then…" He stopped and bit his lip. Harrison got the impression that Colin was not one for public displays of emotion. He was not sure what to say himself, so opted to stay silent and wait for him to continue.

Finally, Colin exhaled and turned his head to Harrison. "Stephanie has always blamed herself, you see. Kids were under her care, and she just took her eye off them for a few minutes. You don't think it'll ever happen to you."

Harrison shook his head in disbelief. "I'm so sorry. I had no idea."

"No, son, you probably wouldn't. Blake was very young when it happened, but as far as I know, it's something he's always kept very close to his chest. It affected him. I don't know how much he actually saw, you know, when it happened, but it changed him as a kiddie. We were so proud when he became a police officer. Having the confidence to go for his dreams like that."

Harrison smiled. "I've always kind of been in a bit of awe as far as Blake's concerned. He pulled me out of quite a dark place, after my parents were arrested. He's just different. He gets people. I guess now I know why."

Colin chuckled. "I couldn't be prouder of how he's turned out, and neither could Stephanie. But that's why she worries so much about him. She wants him to be safe, and happy. But that's why we're here. It's twenty years ago today. She wanted to see him. So did I, if I'm honest with you. But it's different with Stephanie. Her and Blake's relationship has always been a little bit strained because of how much she smothers him sometimes."

It was all starting to make sense, and now Harrison felt even worse for how he had spoken to Blake the night before, and somehow, even more admiration for the man who had not told him to get lost there and then. He was not hurt that Blake had never felt able to tell him about the death of his sister, just sorry that he had to deal with it all on his own, a feeling he knew only too well.

"It would probably be best if we kept this between ourselves, Harrison, lad." Colin put his hand on Harrison's shoulder. "Blake may tell you when he thinks the time is right. But I just wanted you to know why Stephanie can seem a bit…well, you know."

Harrison nodded and smiled. "Don't worry, I will. Thanks, Colin."

"Aye, good lad. And just for the record, I reckon Blake has landed on his feet here. It's a nice village, and he cares about you a lot too. So, don't worry. Anyway, I best be getting back. She'll be waking up soon and I promised to take her to the tea rooms. They're closing down soon, I hear?"

"Yeah," Harrison said, his mind still whirring from what he had been told. "The owners are retiring. I don't think they had anyone to pass it on too, so it's shutting."

"Ah," Colin said, staring into the distance, a wistful look in his eye. "See you around, lad."

"Bye, Colin."

Harrison watched as Colin walked back towards the B&B. In a way, Harrison could see where Blake got his kind hearted nature. Colin was similarly down to earth, and had a twinkle in his eye that Harrison recognised in Blake whenever he was in a good mood. As Betty pulled at the rope, Harrison continued walking, the mental rehearsal of what he was going to say to Blake continuing, but this time, with a very different script.

***

It took Harrison a good half an hour to walk Betty the whole way around the village, having had to stop her from devouring a bed of roses outside the church hall. He was certainly feeling better than he had when he had woken up that morning, but now his mind was preoccupied with how he could make the next day, the anniversary of Bethany's death, as easy for Blake as he could, without giving away the fact that he knew what the day meant to him. He was just walking past the police station, when Betty bleated as the door to the station slamming open startled her. The next moment, a man Harrison had not seen before stormed out, his mobile phone glued to his ear. When he spoke, it was with an American accent, telling Harrison that the man must be Detective Woolf, who Blake had been ranting about. As Harrison stopped on the pavement outside the station to let Betty chew on some dock leaves sticking out of the side of the road, Woolf looked behind him as he spoke urgently into his phone.

"I don't *know* where he is. And I've told you not to call me on this number. But when he turns up, you get in touch with me, in the way we arranged, you hear me?"

Fully aware that he was starting to make a habit of overhearing conversations that he shouldn't, Harrison stepped behind the hedge so that Woolf would not see him.

"I'm not interested in your excuses," Woolf continued, his voice getting lower. "Just do as you're told, and maybe, just maybe, you and your stupid family won't get hurt." He hung up and then pull out a packet of cigarettes, before savagely lighting one. Betty chose that moment to suddenly charge at him, pulling Harrison out of his hiding place. Woolf turned in surprise at the goat and then narrowed his eyes at Harrison.

"Hi," Harrison said nervously. "Sorry about Betty. She's harmless really."

Woolf did not reply. Instead, he glanced at the

hedge where Harrison had come from and was perhaps trying to work out whether Harrison would have been able to hear his phone call or not.

"Is Blake in?" Harrison asked innocently, attempting to distract him.

"Who?" Woolf snapped.

"DS Blake Harte."

"And who are you?"

"I'm Harrison. I'm Blake's boyfriend. I just wondered if he was free for a couple of minutes."

Woolf raised an eyebrow that suggested that Harrison had just met somebody else who was unaware of his relationship with Blake. "No. No, he's not. He's out on a case. Which is exactly where I should be, so if you'll excuse me."

Harrison nodded. He was just about to turn around and pull Betty back the other way when Woolf called back to him from across the road. "Was there a message you wanted me to give your *boyfriend?*"

Harrison thought for a moment. "Just tell him I'm sorry about the misunderstanding last night. I think he'll know what you mean." He gave Woolf a brief smile, then set off back to the cottage.

CHAPTER
NINE

James Pennine was now lying on the ground of the cellar, his eyes staring coldly at the ceiling while the forensics team examined him. The rope he had been found hanging from had been gently coiled from his neck.

Blake and Patil watched as Sharon Donahue, the head of the forensics team, stood up from where she had been crouched over the body and walked towards them. Blake studied her face as she approached and he sighed. "You're going to tell me this isn't as simple as it looks, aren't you?"

Sharon grinned grimly and looked down at the body. "You're saying you found him just hanging from the ceiling when you broke into the room?"

"That's right," Patil said. "Why?"

Sharon bit her lip. "When you hang yourself, the idea behind it is to break your neck, right?" They both nodded. "So," Sharon continued. "Explain to me why his neck isn't broken. As far as I can tell, his neck is bruised from the tightness of the rope, and obviously I'll have to take him back and give him a full examination, but honestly? I don't think he did this to himself."

Blake stared at her for a few seconds and then looked back towards the door they had broken through. Two broken padlocks were on the floor, and a key was still in the lock. "The door was locked. We had to physically kick the door in so we could get in. And now you're telling me that this was *murder*?"

"I can't say anything for sure yet, Blake, you know that," Sharon replied. "All I can tell you is my initial findings. Maybe he was throttled with the rope, and then strung up. It's also worth noting that he's got enough injection marks in his arm to play dot to dot, including one very recent one. He's got traces of vomit 'round his mouth, his lips are blue, his fingernails look black underneath. It's possible that he overdosed on something. Probably heroin. But like I say, I'll have to get him back to make sure."

Blake shook his head in disbelief. "Great. Fantastic. A car that can vanish in the middle of a tunnel, and a man that was too high to know his own name hanging from the ceiling in the middle of a locked cellar."

"A locked cellar that nobody could have got in or out of," Patil added, staring at the padlocks on the ground.

"Anything else?" Blake asked, to nobody in particular, as he stormed out of the cellar.

Patil followed him out, looking confused. "Why was he even here?" she wondered. "I thought we had the Pennines' property nailed as somewhere in Clackton?"

"We do," Blake replied. "Looking at the state of the place, I wouldn't be surprised if we find some of their supplies hidden around somewhere. We'll get it searched. The next question is where the hell is Keith Pennine? They were both in the car last night. And apart from this place, there's nowhere around near where they left it. Unless he was picked up and taken somewhere, but then why was James left here?" His head was beginning to hurt. "None of this makes any sense."

"*Oi!*"

They turned in surprise to where the shrill voice had come from. Striding towards them was a middle-aged woman with greasy hair. Her clothes were filthy, and her eyes were flashing with anger. "What are you pigs doing here? Why don't you leave us alone?"

Blake pulled his ID out of his pocket and held it up as the woman approached. She looked familiar. "Detective Sergeant Blake Harte. Who are you?"

"I ain't telling you *nothin'*," she spat. "Where's Keith? What have you done with him? Or James? Where's my boy?"

Blake remembered her now. "You're Caroline, aren't you? Wife of Keith Pennine and mother of…" he stopped, realising that she clearly had no idea about what they had found in the cellar. Before he could say anything else, the door to the cellar opened, and two men in white coats carried a zipped up body bag out.

Caroline's eyes widened. "Who's in there?"

Blake tried to move her away, but she seemed to take this as confirmation that something terrible had happened. Before anyone could stop her, she had pulled the zip down on the body bag and was staring straight at the cold lifeless face of her son.

"Caroline, come away. Let's go inside," Blake said to her, but instead, Caroline threw her head back and wailed like a wounded animal. Blake hurriedly indicated to the forensics team to take the body away as Patil led Caroline away from them. As Blake walked back into the cellar again, all they could hear was Caroline howling in anguish, demanding to see her son and ask what had happened.

"Try and get the results to me as quick as you can, Sharon," Blake said. "I don't know what the hell has gone on here in the past twenty-four hours, but I'm going to find out, and I'm going to find out quickly."

By the time Patil had managed to calm Caroline down enough to the point where she was able to talk to Blake, Angel had rung ahead and said that he wanted Woolf to be as thoroughly involved with the investigation as possible, especially as it was now looking like a murder enquiry, much to Blake's annoyance. This meant that the interview could not take place until he finally roared into the yard of the house in his silver sports car where Blake was waiting for him. Blake rolled his eyes as the engine of the car died down in front of him. Even though the sun was still perfectly bright in the sky, Woolf had apparently felt the need to raise the headlights on his car, which were on hoods that seemed to sink into the bonnet. Blake had never been one to be impressed by flashy sports cars. He saw them as impractical, as well as too expensive, and the fact that Woolf was the one driving enthralled him even less.

Woolf stepped out of the car and strode towards him. "Harte, what the hell is going on? Angel says you found James Pennine strung up from the ceiling? Suicide?"

"We don't know yet," Blake replied as Woolf walked right past him and towards the house. "And there's still no sign of Keith anywhere. We've got Caroline Pennine though. She's inside. She's just found out her son is dead though, Alec, so we need to go gentle with her."

Woolf turned round, with a disdainful expression on his face. "I don't need to be told how to interview, Harte. She's only got herself to blame, getting mixed up with the likes of Pennine."

Blake jogged to overtake him as he went to open the door to the house and put his hand on the door handle before Woolf could march in. "All the same," he said firmly. "We're not going to get anything out of her at this stage, treating her like a suspect. So, like I say. We go gentle with her."

Woolf sighed and shook his head. "You've heard of the term '*good cop, bad cop*'?"

"Of course."

Woolf moved Blake's hand aside. "Guess which part you'll be playing." Before Blake could answer, Woolf had pushed past him and entered the house. Blake exhaled to calm himself, his fingernails digging into his palms through his clenched fist.

"Urgh," exclaimed Woolf loudly once he was inside, clearly experiencing the smell of the place for the first time. Annoyed as he was, Blake could hardly blame him. The whole house had a strong odour that was a mix of ancient cooking fat and damp mould. The carpets were caked with muck to the point where the original colour was indiscernible, and the walls had an unpleasant brown tinge to them.

They walked into the kitchen, which was no better. There was an almost ceiling high pile of washing up on the side, most of which was covered in green and black mould. Flies were everywhere, and the rubbish bin in the corner had long since over spilt its load, the contents leaking out onto the floor, accompanied by multiple bin liners in a similar state. Blake glanced at Woolf, who had an expression of pure disgust as he glared at Caroline, who was sat at the kitchen table with a small bottle of vodka in her hands.

"Why is she drinking?" Woolf snapped.

"I tried to make her a cup of tea," Patil said, entering from behind. "But could *you* make a cuppa in this kitchen?"

"You should have arrested her and brought her to the station," Woolf argued. "That's what *I* would have done."

"Arrested her for what?" Blake hissed. "Being a bad housekeeper? We've got nothing to charge her with."

Woolf muttered something in reply, then sat down at the table, wincing as he pulled the blackened chair out. Blake sat down beside him, and watched Caroline for a few moments before clearing his throat.

She seemed to barely acknowledge their presence, merely staring right through them. Blake wondered what exactly was going on in her head.

"Caroline?" he prompted gently. "How are you feeling?"

She did not reply. Instead, she took a generous swig of her vodka.

"I don't think that's going to help, do you?" Blake asked her. "Can I just take it from you while we talk?"

Caroline laughed bitterly, before taking an even bigger swig. When the bottle was half empty, she slammed it on the table and pushed it towards Blake, who took it and placed it behind him.

"How am I feeling?" Caroline repeated, her voice slurring slightly. "Just great. Absolutely *fantastic*. How do ya think I feel? I mean you're supposed to be coppers ain't ya? Deal with this all the time. Y'know how I'm feeling. My son's *dead.*"

"Where's Keith?" Woolf asked, sitting with his arms crossed, without a modicum of sympathy. "Don't tell us you don't know where he is."

"I don't," Caroline muttered. "I ain't seen him since yesterday."

"When was that?" Blake asked her, throwing a warning look at Woolf.

Caroline put her head in her hands. "When he went to pick up James from work. That was the last time I saw either of 'em. Far as I knew, it was just a normal day."

"And what did you do after that?"

"I went to work," Caroline replied. "I work nights at the care home in Clackton."

Woolf snorted. "They leave you in charge of the elderly? Wow."

Caroline scoffed at him, but did not reply, something Blake could not help but commend her for. "We've been after Keith and James for a while, Caroline," he said, clasping his hands together. "As I'm sure you're aware."

"Yeah," Caroline spat. "Wouldn't leave us alone. Could never pin anything on 'em though, could ya?"

"We've got you living at another property," Blake continued. "So, what's this place?"

Caroline shrugged. "Just somewhere we were planning on moving too. We were gonna do the place up. We got it cheap."

"I'm not surprised," Woolf retorted waspishly. "I wouldn't pay a dime for this dump."

"Nah, well you wouldn't, would ya?" Caroline replied. "We can't all afford posh sports cars, ya know. Some of us have to work 'ard for what we have."

"So, the drug dealing business isn't what it once was then?" Woolf asked lightly. "I remember a time when guys like Keith would be sunning it up in a villa in Spain somewhere with what they took from it. You guys must have been pretty crappy at it."

"Look," Caroline snapped. "I dunno where Keith is, and my son is lyin' dead in a mortuary somewhere. I wanna see him! I wanna see my boy."

"And you will," Blake replied. "But in the past twenty-four hours, your husband has pulled off the best vanishing trick I've ever seen and as for James, well…" He glanced at Woolf and then Patil, who was stood silently in the corner of the room. "Did he ever seem depressed to you? Was there ever any sign, anything you can think of that suggested to you that he was considering suicide?"

Caroline's eyes filled with tears again and she shook her head. "No."

"What about the amount of drugs he was taking? That can sometimes -"

"My James didn't take drugs, what you on about?"

Blake sighed. "Caroline, we found marks on his arms. There's strong evidence that he was frequently injecting."

"What, you think he was some sort of smackhead? You're worse at this than I thought," Caroline scoffed.

"Then how do you explain the injection marks on his arm?" Blake pressed.

Caroline sighed in exasperation, then stood up and walked across the kitchen to a drawer in the sideboard. She pulled out a box from it and threw it on to the table. Blake and Woolf stared at it in surprise.

"Insulin?" Blake said, his eyebrows raised. "He was diabetic?"

Caroline sat back down and stared back at him

levelly. "The doctors advised him to put it in his arm, he was so skinny." She leant forwards and spoke slowly as if Blake was extremely stupid. "You need a fatty area to put the needle. His arms were about the flabbiest part of him, so that's where he put it."

Blake stared silently at the insulin box on the table, his mind whirring. There was no doubt in his mind now that James had been murdered. He would have to wait for Sharon's forensic report on the body, before he jumped to too many conclusions, but if the cause of death was, as they suspected, a drugs overdose, then it left Blake with more questions than answers as to what exactly the relationship was between James and the drugs that he and his father were known to be supplying to addicts in the local area.

"What about Keith?" Woolf asked, in a tone that he did not quite believe what Caroline was telling them. "You telling me that he was as clean as a whistle too?"

Caroline shuffled uncomfortably in her seat. "I dunno, do I?"

Blake leant forwards in his seat. "I think you do, Caroline."

"I ain't telling you nothing," Caroline replied, pulling a strand of hair out of her eyes, more as a nervous tick than a necessary action.

"Where is he?" Woolf asked, in a low and dangerous voice. "I promise you, it is best for everyone, including you, if you just tell us." He leant forwards and spoke slowly. "*Where is your husband?*"

Caroline held her own, leaning towards him in a mocking manner. "*I don't know.* Now, I wanna see my son."

***

As Patil drove Caroline to identify her son's body, Blake leant against the wall of the house, inhaling on his ecig. It was doing nothing to lessen his cravings. An open packet of cigarettes appeared in front of him.

"Just have one," Woolf implored. "I can tell you want to. The odd one won't hurt you, trust me."

Blake stared at the packet for a few seconds before sighing and taking one. Woolf lit it with his clipper lighter before snapping it shut with a dramatic flourish, puffing away on his own. "Well, I dunno, Harte. This whole thing smells funny to me. A car that vanishes, a drugged up waster hanging himself…" He turned towards Blake, who had gone to interrupt him. "Don't tell me you believe any of that crap she was coming out with, Harte. I saw this sort of thing every day back home. Families pretending that they weren't all screw ups. She's probably out of her mind on something herself, or coming down of it. You're too trusting, Harte."

Blake blew out the smoke, regretting every inhale.

"Let's just say for a minute, that she's telling the truth, and all those marks on his arms *were* just from his insulin jabs, that means that if Sharon does find something else in his system, then it wasn't meant to be there. It makes no sense."

"Exactly," Woolf replied triumphantly. "It makes no sense at all, which is why it's a load of crap. If a suspect tells you something that doesn't make sense, then it isn't true. I learnt that many years ago. I'd have thought you would too."

"So by that logic, we're lying about the car disappearing in that tunnel?" Blake retorted. "Because that sure as hell doesn't make any sense. And Keith is somewhere out there." He wandered towards the open door of the cellar and stepped inside. "And somehow, that car trick and the fact that we've got a hung body in a locked cellar who definitely didn't die from what we're supposed to think he did, leads to here." He looked around the cellar, deep in thought.

"Angel wants us on the same page, Harte," Woolf said sternly from the doorway as Blake paced around the cellar, the sound of the heels from his shoes on the wooden planks on the floor echoing around them. "We can't work together if I'm the only one working with facts instead of fantasy. If we're gonna crack this thing, then I need you *with* me."

"You can't force pieces that don't go together to fit," Blake replied quietly as he looked around the cellar.

"Not everything is straight out of a Conan Doyle novel, Harte. Anyway, I've been thinking about that crazy crap with the car last night."

Blake raised a disdainful eyebrow. "Oh yes?"

"All we saw was the back lights of the Pennines' car, right?"

"Right."

"So obviously, he just turned his back lights off, then hit the gas and put on speed. He must have been out of that tunnel before I managed to get my headlights back on. All we must have seen was the dust he left behind after he had zipped off ahead. Then of course we stopped when we left the tunnel, all confused, and he just kept on driving. It was just our brains playing tricks on us."

Blake stared at him in disbelief. "That *wasn't* what happened, there wasn't time for him to speed off without us seeing him. And anyway, a car like that, surely we'd have heard his engine roaring more if he '*zipped ahead*' as you put it. And, while we're on the subject, you said *your* headlights were smashed when we ran into the back of him. That's exactly what you said."

"So?"

"So, how did you turn them back on?"

"Obviously, they weren't smashed," Woolf replied, shrugging. "We just thought they were when they went out. I got them back on, that's the main thing. Pennine is lucky. If he'd done any damage to that baby, he'd have more than just his son's funeral to pay for. I'll wait for you in the car. Don't be long, Angel's waiting."

Blake nodded vaguely as Woolf left him alone in the cellar. For a few more minutes, Blake wandered around the room, trying to find anything that could give him a clue, ultimately finding nothing. But then, as he was walking back to the car, the details of the interview with Caroline flying around his head, he frowned.

"How did Caroline know you had a sports car?" he asked as he sat down in the passenger seat.

"Huh?" Woolf grunted, as he started the car.

"When she said to you *'we can't all afford posh sports cars.'* How did she know? Have you two met before?"

Woolf stared at Blake for a moment, before his face fell, rolling his eyes. "You're just making this stuff up now, aren't you Harte? Obviously, she saw me arriving through the kitchen window."

"You couldn't see anything out of those windows," Blake retorted, but Woolf cut him off.

"Gimmie a break, Harte." He reversed quickly out of the yard and spun round to face the road. "Just focus on finding Keith Pennine so we can put this whole thing to bed."

"Right," murmured Blake. "I will."

As they drove back to Harmschapel in silence, Blake's mind was anything but quiet. Something was not right, and he was beginning to wonder if whatever it was could be a lot closer than he had first realised.

CHAPTER
TEN

When Blake arrived home that evening, Harrison was waiting for him. Blake was immediately struck when he walked through the front door by how clean the house was. He was then greeted with the unmistakable aroma of pasta, pesto and bacon. Cooking was not one of Harrison's strong points, but he even he was capable of making Blake's favourite comfort food.

"Hey," Harrison said, as Blake walked into the kitchen. He was grating a big block of cheese into a bowl. "I thought you might be hungry."

It was the first time the two of them had spoken since their argument.

"It smells amazing," Blake replied, smiling. "Thanks. Are we okay?"

Harrison didn't say anything, he just pulled the wooden spoon out of the saucepan containing the pasta and pesto, and placed it in Blake's mouth. Blake laughed over the spoon. "Nice. I've taught you well."

Harrison shrugged. "It's not that hard. And yes, we're fine. I'm sorry I acted like such a child."

Blake placed his arms around him and pulled him in. "You didn't. I'm sorry too."

They kissed, and the argument seemed to become a thing that had happened years ago. They were just in danger of forgetting about eating altogether when Blake felt his phone vibrating in his pocket. "Sorry," he mumbled, pulling away. He looked at the screen, praying that it was not someone from the station. "It's Sally. I can ring her back later, it's fine." He went to pull Harrison in again, but found the wooden spoon blocking them; Harrison grinning teasingly.

"Don't worry about it," he said. "Answer it. I've still got to put the garlic bread in. I'll shout you when dinner's ready." He whacked Blake sharply on the backside with the spoon.

"Ow!" Blake exclaimed, rubbing the place where the spoon had hit. He then raised an eyebrow. "And yet…"

Harrison laughed. "Get out of here."

Blake grinned at him and then ran upstairs, answering the phone. "Sally Ann Matthews, as I live and breath."

"Hello, my darling," replied his best friend. "It's been a while. Are you at home?

Blake walked into his bedroom and threw himself on the bed. "Too long. How are you?"

"I'm fine," Sally replied. "I was ringing to see how *you* were. You know, with the time of year and everything."

Blake leant across the bed and pushed the bedroom door closed with his foot. It wasn't that the anniversary of Bethany's death had skipped his mind, but everything that had happened in the past twenty-four hours had distracted him. "Oh yeah, that. I'm alright. Or rather, I would be if my parents hadn't decided to show up out the blue."

"You're kidding me. Oh God. Please tell me your mother hasn't eaten Harrison."

Blake chuckled. "Near as dammit. She found out about everything that went on with his parents. So, obviously, she dealt with the whole thing with an unparalleled amount of tact and diplomacy."

"Oh, the poor boy. I can imagine. Still, though. It's Harrison – I bet he understands, right? I mean, he knows more than anyone what it's like to have a mother who's slightly overboard with the whole protecting her son thing."

Blake glanced at the closed bedroom door. He could just hear Harrison clattering around in the kitchen below. "Well, that's the thing," he said quietly. "I haven't told him."

There was a pause. "What do you mean you haven't told him? Haven't told him what?"

"About Bethany."

"*What?* Why the hell not?"

Blake groaned. "That's the thing, I don't know. I guess it's just because it's personal. Since they've been here, well, Mum more than Dad, I've been thinking about just why I came here to Harmschapel. What exactly I was running away from. Yeah, the whole Nathan thing was a huge part of it, but it was more than that. I needed to just get away and live my own life. I just haven't realised it until recently. In some ways, I guess Nathan did me a favour."

Sally sighed. "I get it, Blake, but why not tell him? It's not like it's some dark secret you've got. It's not *your* parents in prison. It was just a tragic and horrible thing that happened to your family. It's nothing to be ashamed about."

Blake's eyes fell on a picture of him and Harrison on the bedside table. It had been taken soon after they had become an item in The Dog's Tail, both beaming happily at the camera seemingly without a care in the world. "I know."

"And anyway, Blake, I know you too well," Sally scolded. "You think that just because Harrison had so much happen to him to get him to this point that it would be wrong of you to show him that you've got your own skeletons. A time of your life that you find difficult to face up to."

"Maybe," Blake conceded.

"There's no maybe about it," Sally replied sharply. "And you're wrong. You're in a relationship, and this is the sort of thing you need your boyfriend's support with, no matter what your mother might say."

Blake picked up the picture of he and Harrison, and looked at it fondly. He knew Sally was right, and at that moment, he felt stupid for trying to hide anything from Harrison.

The two of them chatted a bit longer, Blake enquiring how things were at his old station, Sally giving him the latest gossip and before he knew it, Harrison had called to him that dinner was ready. Blake was about to end the call when a thought struck him. "Sal, does the name Inspector Alec Woolf mean anything to you?"

"No. Should it?"

"If you ask him, it certainly should," Blake replied dryly. He quickly told Sally about what had been happening over the past couple of days and how Woolf had arrived.

Sally snorted with derision. "He sounds like an absolute tit."

"He is," Blake replied. "But, if you've got a bit of time on your hands, could you find out what you can about him? There's something that doesn't smell right, and it's not just his awful aftershave."

"Anything for you, my darling. Now, go and spend a lovely evening with your man."

"I will. Talk soon."

He ended the call and ran downstairs to find Harrison sitting down at the dining room table, a tall candle lit in the middle between their two plates.

Blake smiled as he sat down. "This looks amazing. Thank you."

"No worries," Harrison replied, blushing slightly. "Sally alright?"

"Yeah," Blake said, helping himself to the garlic bread. "I've asked her to do me a bit of a background check on Woolf. There's something not right about him."

Harrison's eyes widened as he placed a huge forkful of pasta into his mouth. "Hmm! That reminds me," he said, chewing frantically. "I overheard him having a weird phone conv –"

But before he could continue, there was a sharp knock on the front door. They looked at each other for a moment, clearly neither expecting company.

"I'll get it," Blake said, placing his uneaten garlic

bread slice back on his plate. "Whoever it is, I'll try and get rid of them."

He opened the door to find his father standing there. "Alright, son?" he said in his usual gruff voice.

"Dad. We were just having dinner."

Colin sighed and stepped inside. "Your mother wants you. Or rather she wants both of us."

Blake groaned as he closed the door. "Why?"

His father looked at him sternly. "You know why, lad. You know what day it is today."

Blake glanced at Harrison who was watching them both. "Yeah," he said. "I do. She can't just click her fingers and I come running though. Especially when she can't even be bothered to come get me herself. You're not her errand boy, Dad."

"Blake, any other time I'd agree with you, son – but this is important to her. And it's important to me."

"I can't just leave Harrison like this, Dad," Blake said.

"He knows, lad."

Blake raised his eyebrows and stared at Colin. "What do you mean he knows?"

Colin cleared his throat and sat down at the table, swiping the piece of garlic bread off Blake's plate. "I told him about Bethany this morning. So, you don't have to pretend anymore, lad."

Blake turned his head towards Harrison who was busying himself with the pasta on his plate. "Harrison?

Is this true?"

Harrison placed his fork down and looked up at Blake awkwardly. "Well, yeah. He wanted to tell me why your mum had been acting sort of crazy. I didn't say anything, because I figured that you hadn't told me for a reason."

Blake was unsure as to whether he was more annoyed with Colin for telling him before he had had a chance, or with himself for underestimating Harrison's emotional maturity.

Finally, he sighed and shrugged his shoulders. "Fine. I'll come. But Harrison is coming with us."

Colin glanced at Harrison nervously. "Erm, no offence, Harrison, but I don't think that's such a good idea, son."

"Blake, I don't want to cause you any problems. You go. It's only pasta, I don't mind." Harrison added.

"Well, I do," Blake said firmly. "She's got to accept that Nathan is a thing of the past and that Harrison is my present and, I hope, my future as well. As far as I'm concerned, he's as much a part of this family as she thought Nathan was." He walked behind Harrison and placed his hands on his shoulders. Colin still looked reluctant, but finally agreed.

"You're more like your mother than you'd care to admit," he chuckled. "I dunno what she's going to say, but, let's go, before she sends out a search party."

***

When they arrived at the B&B, the sun was setting and the village seemed to be bathed in a warm orange glow. As they walked around the corner, Blake was perturbed and surprised to see a familiar silver sports car parked outside the building.

"Dad?" he exclaimed. "Have you met the driver of this car?"

Colin glanced at the car. "Oh, yeah. Seems like a nice enough fella. Bit up himself, but then, some of those yanks are, aren't they? He was showing me his car. Couldn't stop talking about it, truth be told. I have to say though, she's a beauty." They stopped as Colin stopped and admired the car for a few moments. "I've always wanted one of these. Gorgeous car."

"So, he's staying here?" Blake murmured.

"Aye," Colin replied as they walked into the B&B. "He's a few rooms down from us. He mentioned he was working with you at the station. Full of praise for you, as it goes."

"Really?" Blake said, glancing at Harrison. "You surprise me."

They entered the B&B, Blake and Harrison hand in hand. Blake briefly greeted Nora, the owner. She was sat at the reception desk cuddled up to a cat that appeared to be more fur than animal, with its face just visible through a mane of fluff round it's head.

"Just going up to visit my parents, Nora," he said.

"Alright, my love," Nora replied. She seemed more preoccupied with the cat than who had just entered her establishment. As they climbed the stairs, Blake heard a familiar voice echoing through the corridor.

"Let me tell you, Stephanie – those guys had *nothing* once I'd got them in that interview room. Some cops have it, some don't. They just go to pieces under my questioning."

"Oh, I'm sure," he could hear his mother replying, sounding impressed. "And I must say, it *is* a comfort to know that the public has officers like you on the force"

Blake rolled his eyes as they arrived at the top of the stairs. Woolf was leaning against the doorway of the Hartes' room, Stephanie in front of him, looking far friendlier than she had done at any point since she had arrived in Harmschapel.

"Evening, Mum," Blake said, glancing at Woolf.

"Oh, Blake," Stephanie replied brightly. "Alec here was just telling me all about his work in America. It sounds so *exciting!*" She turned back to Woolf, clearly absorbed. "It must be so *dangerous* with all those guns though."

Woolf shrugged, then in a swift movement with his hand, he flicked a pair of sunglasses he had resting on the top of his head down over his eyes. "It can be. They say cops never have any guarantee that they're ever going to come home from their shifts, but that's more true in the United States. There's more psychos out there than ever before, and we need our guns to protect us. Thank God we got a president in charge who understands that."

Blake stared at Woolf in disbelief. He was chewing gum and the completely unnecessary sunglasses made him look more of an idiot than Blake had previously thought was possible. Somehow, outside of work, Woolf was even more arrogant and the fact that his own mother was feeding this irritated him even further. She normally hated people chewing gum, but apparently Woolf was an exception.

"Anyway," Woolf said, flashing Stephanie a grin. "I'll leave you guys to it. Your son here is a lot of fun to work with. He's got a bit to learn, but we all did once, I guess. Have yourselves a nice evening. See you tomorrow, Harte."

Blake was too annoyed to reply. He just glared at Woolf as he strutted past and into his room a few doors down.

"Such a nice man," Stephanie commented. "What a life he must have led to make the UK Police force want him. Very impressive. Harrison, good evening. What are you doing here?"

Blake took hold of Harrison's hand and gripped it tightly. "He's here with me, Mum. The sooner you realise that Harrison is now part of this family, the happier we'll all be."

Stephanie looked at Blake over her glasses. "Blake,

tonight is not the time for you to be rebelling. We can talk about all this another time. Tonight, of all nights, I'm sure you would not begrudge me a bit of private family time?"

"Harrison knows what today is, Mum," Blake replied hotly. "I'm not keeping it a secret from him anymore." He exchanged a look with Colin. He knew that it was better for his father if Stephanie thought that Blake had been the one to divulge the details, rather than Colin. His father smiled at him gratefully, but Stephanie looked outraged.

"You *told* him?" she murmured. "Blake, I don't want the whole world knowing that I -" She stopped, her lip quivering. When she spoke again, it was with the type of fragility she only tended to have this time of year. "I don't want the whole world knowing *our* private business." She wiped her eyes and looked at him sternly. "Now, please. I'm sorry, Harrison, but I would rather Blake was here on his own. I can assure you that it has nothing to do with our *discussion* yesterday."

She turned on her heels and walked into the room, closing the door smartly behind her. Colin sighed and shrugged his shoulders. "You tried, lads. Come on, Blake. Harrison, I'm sorry."

"No, I'm not having her -"

"Blake," Harrison said, pulling him away from the door. "Listen to me."

As Colin followed Stephanie into the room, Harrison held on to Blake's arm and pulled him back. "Look, you go. I don't need to be here. There's no point in me upsetting your mum at a time like this."

"I *want* you to be here," replied Blake, taking hold of his hand.

"I know, and I want to be here too," Harrison said. "But let's be honest, I'm only here *really* to prove a point. We've got three hundred and sixty-four other days of the year to do that. Let her have tonight with just you. Once tonight's over and done with, then we can concentrate on the whole you and me thing."

Blake looked up at the door his father had just disappeared through and sighed, before kissing Harrison softly on the forehead. "You, Harrison Baxter, are wiser than you give yourself credit for."

Harrison grinned and gave a small shrug. "I know. You have no idea how much pasta and pesto I'm going to eat tonight. And all the garlic bread."

Blake laughed loudly and gave his boyfriend a tight hug. "Enjoy. I'll be back tonight."

"Alright, see you later."

Blake kissed him again, then walked into his parents' room. His mother had prepared a meal and was pouring wine into three glasses. She looked up as Blake entered, alone.

"Thank you," she said. "Now, take a seat. Nora, that nice lady downstairs with the ugly cat, she let me use the oven in the kitchen. Tuck in."

Despite how annoyed he was with her, Blake's stomach was now aching from hunger after not eating a bite of the meal Harrison had made, so he sat at the table. Once they were all sat down, Stephanie held up her wine glass. "To Bethany."

Blake glanced at his father, who winked at him. Then, they all chinked their wine glasses together. "To Bethany."

As they ate, none of them had any way of knowing the danger that Harrison was about to find himself in.

CHAPTER
ELEVEN

Outside in the corridor, Harrison was feeling good about himself. He felt he had made the right decision in telling Blake to go in on his own, and was hoping that it would go some way to showing Stephanie that he was good for her son. As he made his way back towards the stairs, he heard Woolf's voice.

"Look, I'll deal with Harte, you just concentrate on finding that dumb husband of yours."

Harrison frowned at hearing Blake's name, forcing him to turn back towards Woolf's room.

"How am I supposed to know where he is?" Woolf continued angrily. "You can quit the waterworks, I know you too well and I *know* when you're lying to me. I had your back at that interview in that *disgusting* place you call a house, but if you keep feeding me BS, then I promise you that you're on your own."

Harrison guessed that Woolf was talking on his phone, and though he only knew the sketchiest of details regarding Blake's case, it sounded like there was more going on under Blake's nose than he thought. He pressed himself against the wall by the door and listened intently.

"I don't believe you, Caroline. Come on, you owe me. If it wasn't for me, both Keith and James would be in a cell." There was a pause, before Woolf snapped again angrily, "Of *course* I'm having trouble with Harte, you stupid woman! Y'know this crummy B&B I'm staying in? His parents are just two rooms across from me, and Harte himself, and that weedy little boyfriend of his, have just turned up. So yeah, to answer your question, Harte *is* becoming a problem." He stopped for a few moments. Harrison was just starting to wonder if Woolf had hung up when there was suddenly the sound of a loud and forceful inhalation. Harrison frowned again. It sounded like Woolf had just sniffed something loudly. He then heard Woolf gasp and curse, before continuing his conversation. "And you wonder why I take this stuff.

Yeah, I know you're going through a tough time right now, Caroline, and I'm sorry about James and whatever, but he brought that on himself." Another pause. "Don't give me that crap about how clean he was. Let's be real – he took after his Dad, right? Just stay at the house, I'm on my way to you. Course I'm alright to drive like this, I've been doing it for years."

Harrison heard movement behind the door. Looking around frantically for somewhere to hide, he spotted a cleaning cupboard a couple of doors down. Praying that it was unlocked, he dived across the corridor and pulled the door handle. It opened, just as Woolf's door flung open and he stepped out, taking the stairs at a run. Harrison watched him leave through the gap in the cleaning cupboard door then stepped out. He debated whether it would be appropriate to tell Blake what he had heard; He did not imagine Stephanie would be too thrilled about them being interrupted again. Deciding it would be best to text Blake, allowing him to deal with it later, Harrison pulled his mobile out of his pocket. Then, he realised that the door to Woolf's room was still ajar. Harrison's heart skipped a beat. He knew that Blake would probably have loved the chance to investigate that room given half a chance. Harrison crept to the end of the corridor and looked down the stairs. Woolf was nowhere to be seen. Checking one more time that the coast was clear, Harrison entered the room.

Unlike the room that the Hartes were currently in, Woolf's single room was quite small. A large rucksack that had clothes spilling out of it was lying on the floor. Harrison rummaged through it. Aside from the clothes, the rucksack was filled with the usual assortment of odds and ends, a bathroom bag filled with a razor, toothpaste and toothbrush, and aftershave, an array of boxer shorts and socks, and a mobile phone charger. But there were also several magazines, all of them with flash cars on the front. One particularly frayed copy that Harrison pulled out had a makeshift bookmark in it. Opening it to the page, Harrison was surprised to see an article under the heading "*Cars from the 90s.*" The car that had been chosen for that week's article did not looks especially impressive. It looked like the sort of car that was cheap and common around any number of roads in the country, though Harrison was not clued up enough to know anything else about the "*Accord Aerodeck.*" Even more strangely, was a picture of the back of the car. It was not so much the picture itself that confused Harrison, it was the fact that whoever had been reading the magazine, presumably Woolf, had circled the picture of the rear of the car in red ink. Harrison placed the magazine back in the rucksack and looked around the rest of the room. Immediately, he spotted another magazine on the bed. It was a top shelf '*lad's mag*' with a buxom blonde woman on the cover, pouting at the camera wearing very little aside from a skimpy set of underwear. But on the magazine's cover was a very tightly rolled up twenty-pound note, next to which was a very small plastic bag containing what looked to Harrison like white powder. It was this substance which Harrison had presumably heard Woolf inhaling before. Harrison thought back to what he had heard Woolf saying on the phone. *'And you wonder why I take this stuff.'*

The fact that Woolf clearly had some sort of serious drug problem, and that he clearly knew how the car in the tunnel had disappeared, was enough for Harrison to decide that he needed to let Blake know right away. He turned to leave the room and gasped loudly; Woolf was standing right in front of him, blocking the door. His eyes were narrowed, flashing with anger.

"Oh dear," he growled as he slammed the door closed. "Now, what am I going to do with *you*?"

Harrison backed away, his eyes wide. He opened his mouth to shout for Blake, but before the words had even left his lips, Woolf had picked up a lamp from the bedroom cabinet and swung it around. Then, everything went black.

ROBERT INNES

CHAPTER TWELVE

Blake woke up the next morning face down on the sofa in Juniper Cottage. It took him a few seconds to realise what had woken him up. Betty the goat was butting the back door, angrily glaring at Blake through the glass.

"Shut up you *stupid* animal," Blake murmured.

He rubbed his head and groaned. The red wine his mother had insisted on repeatedly pouring into his glass had given him the most horrendous hangover. The night had gone on far longer than Blake had intended, mostly because Stephanie had gotten so drunk, she had become emotional. By the time Blake and his father had calmed her down and put her to bed, it had been almost two in the morning. So, when Blake arrived home, he decided to sleep on the sofa so that he did not wake Harrison up.

He looked up at the clock on the wall and was horrified to see that he had to be at work in five minutes. With no time to shower, he quickly put on the clothes that he had haphazardly thrown on the armchair the night before, and grabbed his keys off the table, grateful that he had had the sense to throw them somewhere visible before he had passed out on the sofa. As he was leaving, he realised that the dining room table was still set up from dinner the night before. Both bowls were still full of pasta, and the garlic bread that Colin had taken a bite out of was still lying untouched on Blake's plate. Blake stared at it for a few moments, but he did not have time to consider the matter. He decided that Harrison must have been tired and gone to bed early without eating it, and hurried out of the cottage.

***

"Before you all begin today," Angel announced in the meeting room. "I have had a call from Detective Woolf. He's unwell so won't be in today. He has asked me to pass on his apologies, and he hopes to be back with us tomorrow. Now then, carry on."

The team gave a brief murmur of acknowledgment and continued with what they were doing. Angel then turned around in the doorway to his office, his skeletal frame barely filling the gap. "DS Harte? A brief word, if I may?"

Blake, who had been trying to stifle a long yawn while Angel had been speaking was caught off guard and turned to him with his mouth wide open. Ignoring Mattison laughing at him, he followed Angel into his office and closed the door behind them. "Sir?"

Angel sat down at his desk and smiled brightly up at him. "I was just wondering how you're getting on with Detective Woolf?" Blake was not entirely sure on how to answer. He certainly saw no point in informing Angel about any of his suspicions regarding his new colleague, especially as he did not actually have any evidence to support them. Angel seemed to notice his hesitation. "DS Harte?"

"Well, let's just say I find him slightly *unorthodox*, Sir."

"In what way?"

"We haven't made a huge amount of progress on the case."

Angel raised an eyebrow. "Considering one of the suspects has turned up dead, I don't think you can really call it the same case, do you?"

Blake bit his lip. He did not feel up to bandying details with Angel at this moment.

"I had heard nothing but good things from any superior that Detective Woolf has worked under," Angel continued. "Are you trying to tell me that *they* are incorrect?"

Blake sighed. "He can be difficult, Sir. *I* find him difficult anyway. Perhaps me and him just have different ways of working."

"Difficult, how?"

Blake considered how was best to word his answer. "I find our personalities clash. Maybe we're both just very used to our own way of working."

"Could it be that you feel like he is treading on your toes?"

Blake stared at him. "I'm sorry?"

"Just as I say," Angel replied. "I have invited this well recommended detective to work with us, and you feel like he is taking over, that the other officers are looking up to him a bit too much?"

"Considering that I don't think the other officers like him that much either, no, I don't think that, *Sir,*" Blake shot back. "Now, if there was nothing else, I've got a team meeting."

Angel narrowed his eyes for a few moments, looking thoughtful, then waved his hand to indicate that Blake was free to leave. Blake wrenched open the door to the office, and had to use every fibre in his being to prevent him from slamming it loudly behind him.

"Okay, listen up," he said sharply as he strode to the front of the room. "I'd like us to try and go over what we know, what we think, and what our next move is. Everyone here?" His eyes darted round the room to check that everyone he needed was present and then continued as the room fell quiet. "Right. Since our last meeting, which was led by the delightful Detective Woolf..." The scribbled notes that Woolf had scrawled on the white board were still facing the room, so Blake swiftly pulled the board down to reveal his own notes from a previous meeting, then continued. "... we have somehow lost one suspect." He picked up the board marker and drew a line away from James' name. "James Pennine was found dead in an old house just on the outskirts of Harmschapel. He was hanging from the ceiling of a cellar located on the property. Do we have the forensic report?"

"Got it here, Sir," Patil said, passing him the file. Blake rummaged through it till he found the picture of James' body that had been taken at the scene.

"So, as we can see from the lacerations round the neck, his body was found with the rope tied tightly around it, however, Sharon does not believe that's what killed him. She's confirming in her report that he died from an overdose of heroin." He pulled another picture from the file. It was a close up on an injection mark on James' arm. "Okay, what we have here is the wound that Sharon believes was where this lethal dose of heroin was injected."

"I thought he had quite a few injection marks on his arm? Hardly surprising, coming from *that* family," put in Gardiner.

Blake held up the forensic report. "Seems that the story Caroline gave us about James being a diabetic who frequently injected insulin was true. If you look at his arm, those aren't track marks. If James was a constant user of heroin, we'd expect to find bigger and more obvious entry wounds, but she believes that these were made by an insulin needle."

"So, we don't even have a murder weapon?" Mattison clarified.

"Certainly looks that way," Blake replied. "And of course, just for fun, the room we found James in was locked from the inside, with padlocks and a big old key that was still in the lock. So, what we've got to ask ourselves is who would want to murder him?"

"That's not exactly difficult, is it?" Gardiner scoffed. "We're talking about the Pennines here. We've been after them for months. We obviously weren't the only ones. These drug addicts make enemies."

"You're missing the point, Michael," Blake replied. "James was not a drug addict. He was maybe helping his Dad with the dealing and everything else, but according to the post mortem, insulin was about the most toxic drug he ever put into himself."

"So what?" Gardiner insisted. "Maybe some lowlife used him to get to his dad? You're not trying to tell me Keith bloody Pennine was as pure as the driven snow?"

"I can't tell you *anything* about Keith bloody Pennine," Blake said bitterly, turning around to face the board again. "Because Keith bloody Pennine has apparently vanished off the face of the earth. Which brings us to *this!*" He produced the photo of the burnt out car and placed it onto the board.

"Ah yes." Gardiner smirked. "The car you and your new best friend managed to lose in the middle of a tunnel. Very careless."

"Shut up, Michael," Blake replied. "But, as you say, this car, a crimson Honda Accord Aerodeck, managed to completely evaporate in the middle of Clifton Moore tunnel. About a mile further down the road, the car was then found burnt out in the middle of a field. I would welcome any suggestions."

The room went silent again. Blake glanced around at the perplexed faces.

"It's impossible," Mattison said at last. "There's absolutely no way for it to have vanished in the way you say it did."

"He's right, Sir," Patil added. "It doesn't make any sense."

"I *know* he's right, Mini," Blake replied hotly.

"But it doesn't make it any less true."

"I looked into the history of the tunnel," Patil said, opening her notebook. "To see if there was any construction work done on it recently."

"And?"

"The last time any work was done of the Clifton Moore tunnel was in 1999 when the foundations were checked for any damage following a flood. Apart from that, it hasn't been touched since."

"They couldn't go under it," Gardiner said. "They couldn't go over it, so they had to have gone through it."

"Are you absolutely sure that they didn't just put on an extra burst of speed before the headlights on Detective Woolf's car came back on?" Patil asked. "It's the only thing that makes any sense."

Blake sighed and stared at the photo of the burnt out car. He could hardly blame them for being sceptical. If he had not witnessed it himself, he would have been asking exactly the same questions.

"We were chasing the Pennines in Woolf's car," he said slowly, more to himself than anybody else. "We were going at high speed, it was dark, the rain was lashing down. The tunnel was approaching. Maybe a couple of hundred metres before the entrance to the tunnel, the Pennines' car slowed down, and we rammed into the back of them, which Woolf originally thought had smashed his headlights because we were then thrown into complete darkness. The rear lights on *their* car then went out. Then we entered the tunnel. A few seconds later, their rear lights came back on again, and then so did ours. When ours came back on, we were in the middle of the tunnel and the road in front of us was completely clear. Their car had disappeared. The road in the tunnel is too narrow for us to have accidently overtaken them. There were no secret holes or anything in the road or the walls surrounding us." He stared at the board in front of him. His head was aching, but slowly, an idea was starting to form in his head. He had absolutely no way of proving it, but there was *one* conceivable way that it could have been achieved.

"Where were you even chasing them from anyway?" Gardiner asked, breaking into his thoughts.

Blake snapped his fingers and turned around to face them. "The petrol station on the other side of the village. And that's exactly where me and you are going right now, Michael. Get your coat."

ROBERT INNES

CHAPTER THIRTEEN

The petrol station seemed just as deserted when they arrived as it had done when Blake and Woolf had been watching it on the night they had pursued the Pennines. When they walked in, the woman behind the counter was slouched over it, flicking through the pages, looking bored. When she glanced up and spotted Blake and Gardiner, she looked surprised to see that she actually had some customers.

"Hiya," she said, throwing the magazine aside. "What pump number, please?"

"We haven't come about petrol," Blake replied, producing his ID. "Detective Sergeant Blake Harte, this is Sergeant Michael Gardiner. We're actually here to ask you or anyone who works here some questions about James Pennine?"

The girl scoffed. "Don't talk to me about him right now. I wasn't supposed to be in today, they had to call me in. He's a no show." She looked over her shoulder and leaned in further. "Between you and me, they're not bothered. I had plans today, but they don't care here. So long as the management don't have to get up off their arses. I'm looking for another job."

"There's actually a very good reason James didn't show up for his shift today," Blake replied. "I'm afraid we've got some bad news."

"If you could persuade whoever is your manager today to *'get up off their arse,'* we need to speak to them," Gardiner added from behind Blake.

The woman appeared dumbfounded for a second but quickly ran out the back. As she went, Blake looked at Gardiner and shook his head in disbelief at his lack of tact.

"What?" Gardiner asked.

Before Blake could reply, the woman returned with a man wearing a shirt and tie.

"Good morning," he said. "I'm Nick Brown, manager. Sophie says you wanted to speak to me?"

"Hi, Nick," Blake said. "I'm sorry to have to

inform you that we found the body of James Pennine yesterday."

Nick stared at Blake, his eyes wide. "Are you kidding me? James? Are you sure?"

Blake nodded. "I'm very sorry."

"Oh my God," Sophie gasped, slapping her hand over her mouth. "That's awful. He was such a nice guy! What happened to him?"

Blake was not entirely sure that Sophie was going to be much help, so he asked Nick if there was somewhere more private they could talk.

Once in the back office, Blake and Gardiner sat opposite him. They could see Sophie on the screens of the security cameras. Despite her initial grief, she seemed to have gone back to her magazine.

"We were wondering if you could tell us anything that might help us," Blake said to Nick, who had sat down, looking shaken. "We think he was murdered."

"*Murdered?*" Nick repeated. "My god. The poor guy. I mean, for what it's worth, I've got nothing but good things to say about him. He was a good bloke. Bit of a Jack the Lad, he could be a bit lazy around here, but then look at what I've got in today."

Blake nodded. "Did he give the impression of somebody who might have dabbled with drugs in the past?"

Nick raised his eyebrows in surprise. "Not that I ever saw. He came in hungover a couple of times, but name me someone who hasn't done that at work."

Blake smiled briefly, as his own head throbbed. "Did you ever come across his father, Keith?"

"Yeah," said Nick, his face dropping. "In fact, he's barred from here."

"Why?"

"He's come in a couple of times, off his head. Shouting the odds, causing trouble for James."

"'*Off his head?*' repeated Gardiner. "What do you mean?"

"Drunk," Nick told him. "Though in all honesty, if you're looking for someone who was mixed up with drugs, Keith would probably be your man. I'm no expert, but he often looked like he was on something to me. Weird behaviour, out of nowhere aggression, that sort of thing. But James was nothing like him. In fact, I rather got the impression that he was saving up to move out of his parents' house. I mean, he was only sixteen, but when you're surrounded by that as a family, who can blame him?"

"We do have evidence and witnesses saying that he was involved in drug dealing with Keith," Blake replied.

"Really? Well, I don't know," Nick said. "All I can tell you is that that surprises me. I mean, from what I've heard, Keith could be quite violent and threatening. Maybe he was forcing James into it?"

Blake looked at Gardiner who just shrugged. The

idea of Keith intimidating his son into helping him with his own dealings certainly fit the theory that James was more of an innocent part of proceedings, but at this stage, that was still all it was; a theory.

"Alright, thank you," Blake said, standing up. "If you think of anything else, anything at all that might be of help to us, get in touch with the station."

"Of course," Nick said. "It's all such a terrible shock."

Blake and Gardiner were just on their way out the office when Nick said, "Oh, there was one other thing. The other day, some bloke came in looking for James. I don't know if it's any good to you. I'd never seen him before."

"What bloke was this?" Blake asked him.

"I think he was American," Nick replied. "Older guy. He just asked if James was available, but he was out on his break. I asked if he wanted me to try and get hold of him, but he said it didn't matter and walked out."

Blake turned to Gardiner. "An American man? Can I see him on the cameras?"

"Sure," Nick said. "Won't be a sec."

After a few clicks on the computer, Nick had got up the previous day's footage up on the computer. "And he turned up about half past twelve. There he is."

Blake looked at the screen. There, standing by the

counter talking to Nick was Woolf. "Can I get a copy of this?"

***

Clutching a CD with the footage of Woolf in the petrol station burnt on it, Blake turned to Gardiner as they walked back to the car. "I *knew* there was something not right about Woolf. Why was he here? He said nothing to me about having been here earlier on in the day when we were sat waiting for James to come out."

"So what?" Gardiner replied. "He's a detective, brought here to investigate two people under suspicion of supplying class A drugs. Maybe he went to interview James before he was given instructions by Angel."

Blake pulled his mobile out of his pocket and quickly found Harrison's number. "No. There's something very strange going on with Inspector Woolf, and I'm going to find out what it is."

"Who are you ringing?" Gardiner asked him as they climbed into the car, rolling his eyes.

"Harrison," Blake replied. He had remembered that Harrison had been trying to tell him something about Woolf before Colin had arrived the previous night but the call immediately went to his answer machine. "Where the hell is he?"

"Maybe Inspector Woolf has kidnapped him?"

Gardiner replied cheerfully. "You know what your problem is?"

Blake hung up the phone and stared out in the distance, his mind racing.

"You're jealous. Inspector Woolf has come in and he knows the job, and he's got a huge list of accomplishments behind him. You just don't like that you aren't the big man in the station anymore." He started the car, clearly pleased that he had managed to get that off his chest.

"You're wrong, Michael," Blake replied. "And anyway, you want to talk about jealousy? Let's discuss how you were with me when I first arrived in Harmschapel."

Gardiner's smirk quickly disappeared.

"Right, take us to the house where we found James' body."

"Why?" Gardiner replied sulkily.

"Because," Blake said, his eyes narrowing. "I think we've all been taken for a ride. And we're going to find out exactly what has been happening."

ROBERT INNES

CHAPTER
FOURTEEN

Harrison squinted up from the boot of the car at his captor. The sunlight seemed to sear his eyes, and he could not move his hands to shield them.

"Oh, good," Woolf said, sounding slightly surprised. "You're awake. *Move.*" He grabbed Harrison by the shoulder and dragged him out of the car. Harrison gasped in pain as Woolf picked him up and frogmarched him along the gravel path he had felt the car arriving in. Immediately, Harrison's muscles cried out, aching worse than he had ever felt. However long he had been asleep, or unconscious, in the back of Woolf's car had forced him to lay in an uncomfortable position for too long and his legs immediately gave way.

"*Get up!*" Woolf growled. "Do *not* kid with me right now." He poked the gun into Harrison's ribs sharply, causing him to gasp in pain again. "I said *move.*"

He led Harrison towards a house that looked like it had seen far better days. The yard was covered in overgrown weeds, and the house itself looked filthy. Before Woolf had even reached the front door, a deeply unpleasant smell hit Harrison's nose. He must have reacted because Woolf chuckled bitterly. "Yeah, sorry about this. It's not the cleanest of places." He banged sharply on the door with the butt of the gun and held Harrison tighter, apparently forgetting that both Harrison's feet and hands were tied, so he could not run anywhere even if he could escape Woolf's grasp.

After a few moments, the door opened and a woman stood before them. Her hair looked unwashed, and she was smoking a cigarette that had nearly burnt down to the butt. She looked at Harrison in bewilderment. "Who the 'ell is this? And *what* are you doin' with that thing?" She waved her hand at the gun, her eyes wide as if it might explode at any moment.

"You've got a house guest," Woolf replied curtly,

pushing his way past the woman with Harrison. "Just while I think what to do with him. Don't give me that look, Caroline. I'm really not in the mood."

Caroline closed the door sharply behind them and shook her head. "I don't believe you! Who is he? What's he supposed to 'ave done?"

Woolf gripped Harrison's arm tightly behind his back. "He was sticking his nose in my private business, weren't you? I guess you kind of see why him and Harte go so well together."

Caroline recoiled in horror. "*What?* He's with Harte? That's the copper's boyfriend? Are you off your 'ead? What you bringin' him 'ere for?"

"Because I caught him rifling through my room. He's seen stuff. Too much stuff. I had to do *something!*"

"What, so you brought him *'ere?* Haven't I got enough on me plate right now?" Caroline shouted back.

"I had to think of something!" Woolf snapped. "If he gets back to his boyfriend and tells them what he's seen, then everything is screwed. You, me, and that dumb husband of yours. Then you'll be mourning your son while you're rotting in some cell somewhere. Is that what you want?"

Caroline stared at them both in horror, clearly unsure as how to respond. All the while, Harrison had not said a word. He had been trying to remember what he had seen in Woolf's room, and it was slowly coming back to him. He had found drugs, the sort of drugs that could end Woolf's career in a heartbeat. But was that all that Woolf was worried about? What else could he have found that meant that Woolf felt he had no other option than to hold him captive like this?

Suddenly, they heard the sound of a car. Caroline ran to the window and looked through it, gasping loudly. "It's *him*!" she shrieked. "It's that copper! It's Harte!"

"Jesus," Woolf snapped. "What the hell is he doing here?" He grabbed Harrison by the shoulder and jabbed him with the gun. "Listen to me. You make a sound, then both you and lover boy will find yourselves with a round of bullets inside you, do you hear me?"

"Yeah," Harrison murmured, before Woolf dragged him to the kitchen and opened the door to a pantry. He pushed Harrison inside and then squeezed himself in beside him, slamming the door behind them. As they heard a knock at the front door, Woolf whispered menacingly into Harrison's ear. "One sound and you're dead. Good job I parked 'round the back of the house. Even Sherlock Holmes out there won't know we're here."

"Why are you doing this?" Harrison whispered, more out of fear than because Woolf had told him to be quiet.

"Haven't you learnt anything from the last time you tried poking your nose into my business?" Woolf hissed. "Now, *quiet.*"

Then, Harrison heard Blake's voice. It was the most comforting thing he had ever heard, and yet tears welled up in his eyes. Blake had no way of knowing that Harrison was merely a few feet away, with a gun pointing into his back.

"Caroline, you've met my sergeant, Michael Gardiner."

"What's this about?" Caroline snapped. "I'm busy."

"Not busy cleaning up, I'm guessing?" Harrison heard Gardiner mutter. Even the voice of Michael Gardiner was a comfort to him right now.

"This isn't about James," Blake continued. "I want to ask you a couple of questions, about a colleague of mine, Alec Woolf."

"Who?" Caroline asked hesitatingly. Harrison could only hope that Blake was not fooled by her poor acting.

"The American officer that was with me when we spoke the other day after finding James' body," Blake replied. "I need to know this, Caroline, I need you to be honest. Have you ever met Inspector Woolf before?"

"Oh, you bastard, Harte," Woolf murmured darkly.

Caroline had apparently not responded quick enough for Blake. "Caroline? Had you previously met Alec Woolf before the death of your son?"

"No," Caroline replied sharply. "Course not. What would I 'ang around with coppers for?"

"Caroline," Blake said slowly. "Let me make this clear – if I find you're withholding information from me, you're going to find yourself in a lot of trouble, and I know that's the last thing you need right now."

"Get rid of him, you dumb bitch," Woolf growled quietly.

"I don't know anythin'!" Caroline shouted. "Can you leave me alone? You should be out there trying to find whoever killed my boy! Not here asking me stupid questions."

"I'm inclined to agree," Gardiner drawled. "We're wasting time."

"That Gardiner is good, isn't he?" Woolf whispered. "So much more cooperative than your stupid boyfriend."

Harrison ignored him as he heard Blake sigh. He could just picture the thoughtful look on Blake's face and was praying that he could tell that Caroline was lying.

"Have you heard from Keith?" Blake asked at last.

"No, I told ya, I dunno where he is," Caroline told him.

"Right. Well, if you hear anything, we need to

know. It's really important that we speak to him."

"Yeah, alright!" she snapped.

There was a pause then Harrison heard footsteps walking away from them before they heard the door close. Soon, Caroline had opened the pantry door. "They're gone."

"Good girl," Woolf said. He grabbed her by the waist and kissed her on the cheek. Harrison could not help but notice that she looked absolutely repulsed. Woolf did not seem to notice. He just glared into the distance. "He's getting too close. I need this finished." He turned to Harrison with a horrible smile. "Maybe this has all worked out for the best. I think all Harte needs to back off from this is a bit of gentle persuasion."

ROBERT INNES

CHAPTER
FIFTEEN

"Just drop me off at home, would you?" Blake asked Gardiner. "I'll meet you back at the station."

"I'm not a taxi service, you know," Gardiner grumbled. But nevertheless, he stopped the car outside Juniper cottage.

"And Michael," Blake said as he got out the car. "Please, can I trust you to keep what we've found out today to yourself? I don't want Angel finding out for now."

Gardiner raised a disdainful eyebrow. "You want

me to keep the fact that you've been trying to pin something on Detective Woolf a secret?"

"Just for now," Blake said. "*Please.* It won't be for long. Caroline was lying, even you must be able to see that."

Gardiner did not reply. He just merely shrugged then nodded.

"Thank you. I won't be long."

Blake slammed the door closed and jogged towards the cottage as Gardiner drove away. Harrison would be home by now, and if he knew something that could help Blake, then he needed to know as soon as possible.

"Harrison?" he called as he opened the door. But then he stopped and stared at the dining room table. It was still in exactly the same state as it had been the previous night, untouched. He pulled his mobile out of his pocket and rang the shop where Harrison worked. His stomach sank as Jai Sinnah informed him that Harrison had not been in work that day, and did he know how busy he had been with only him working all evening.

"Where the hell are you, Harrison?" Blake murmured to himself. He tried ringing Harrison again, but his mobile was still switched off.

After checking upstairs to see if he was in bed asleep, or ill, and seeing nobody there, Blake's heart began to thump. As he ran out the cottage and made his way quickly towards the station, he rang his father.

"Dad," he panted breathlessly when Colin answered. "Have you seen Harrison?"

"Harrison? No, not since last night, son," Colin replied. "Is something wrong?"

"I don't know where he is," Blake said. "He's not been to work, and he's obviously not been home either."

"Try not to panic, lad," Colin said. "He seemed alright when we left him in the corridor last night. Maybe he's in the pub?"

"Right, thanks," Blake replied hurriedly and hung up the phone as he arrived at the station. The streetlights outside flicked on as dusk fell over the village, and they weren't the only lights shining in the street. Woolf's silver sports car had its hooded headlights up, beaming down the street with the engine running. Blake stopped and stared at the car. Something had been bothering him about the course of events ever since the meeting earlier that day and now, as he slowly walked towards Woolf's car, he realised what it was. Something that was there now and that hadn't been on the night of the chase. Woolf looked up as Blake approached and flashed him a grin. "Harte. How's it going?"

"Ah, DS Harte." Angel's head poked out of the passenger side window before Blake could reply. "Detective Woolf was just showing me his car. Quite an impressive vehicle, I must say. You really must take me for a spin in it, Alec. I've always had a bit of thing for a sports car." He looked at Blake and smiled. "Boys and their toys, I suppose."

Blake nodded vaguely and turned to Mattison and Patil who were just leaving the station together. "Guys, have you seen Harrison anywhere? I've not seen him since last night and I'm getting a bit worried."

Patil and Mattison looked at each other. "No, Sir, sorry," Patil said, shaking her head. "But if we come across him, we'll tell him to get in touch with you."

Blake's heart sank. He was now starting to panic. It was not like Harrison to just vanish like this.

"Oh, by the way, Sir," Mattison said as he and Patil started to walk away. "There was a letter delivered for you. I think Mandy put it under the reception desk."

"Alright, thanks," Blake said quietly. He glanced back at Woolf who was sitting on the boot of his car with his arms crossed, smugly watching Angel who was still in the passenger seat. For a moment, Woolf's eyes met Blake and his smirk faltered slightly, into an expression that seemed darker somehow. Blake held the look as he walked into the station. It had almost felt like Woolf knew something.

He leant over the reception desk until his hands landed on an envelope. As he pulled it out, he frowned. The letter felt thin and yet had a printed label on the front. *"DETECTIVE SERGEANT BLAKE HARTE. HARMSCHAPEL POLICE STATION."*

Blake walked back outside again, clutching the letter. He was mentally exhausted after the long day, and the hangover he had woken up with that morning had now just left him feeling drained. He would check the pub for Harrison; he was bound to be there.

As he walked towards Woolf's silver sports car, he ripped open the envelope. "I'm going to call it a night, Sir," he said to Angel, who was in the process of opening Woolf's glove compartment. "I think I need to…" But then he stopped as he pulled the letter out of the envelope and took in it's contents. It was all in large capital letters on a single piece of A4 paper. The words made Blake's blood run cold:

"I HAVE HARRISON. IF YOU WANT TO SEE HIM AGAIN, MEET ME AT THE CLIFTON MOORE TUNNEL AT SEVEN. JUST YOU. DON'T TRY ANYTHING, OR HE WILL DIE IN FRONT OF YOU."

"Harte?" Woolf was looking at him, frowning. "What's wrong with you?"

Blake slowly passed him the letter. Woolf read it and bit his lip. "Holy crap," he murmured. He glanced over his shoulder where Angel still seemed preoccupied then turned back to Blake and looked at his watch. "It's nearly seven now. I'll take you," he said quietly. "I'd bet on my Mom's life that Keith Pennine must be behind this. We better not let Angel know for now, in case this guy really does mean business. He could be bluffing, but who knows?" He turned around and faced Angel who had climbed out the passenger seat and was watching them with his eyes narrowed.

"Is there a problem, gentlemen?"

"Not at all, Sir. Harte and me are just going to go have another look at that tunnel. Y'know, in case we missed something. Harte, get in."

Blake did not reply. He merely walked around the car, and sat in the passenger seat. His palms had started to sweat and his heart was thumping in his chest.

"I see, very well," Angel replied. "I have some paperwork to be getting on with, so I'll be here for another couple of hours yet. Inform me of anything you find before you leave, won't you?"

"Of course, Sir," Woolf replied. And without another word, he climbed into the car and he and Blake sped off in the direction of Clifton Moore tunnel.

"Best we leave him out of it for now," Woolf said grimly. "If this is Keith Pennine, then we need to be careful. I'll keep out of sight when we get there. But trust me, Harte. I'll be watching. I've got your back. He's going to be okay."

Blake nodded. "Oh, I'm sure you'll be watching. This ends tonight."

SPOTLIGHT

***

When they arrived at the tunnel, night had well and truly drawn in, and like the last time they were here at this time, the only light on the road ahead was the headlights from Woolf's car. Woolf slowed down and drove into the passing spot a few metres from the tunnel. Then he turned off the ignition, and the car subsided into silence as they were plunged into near pitch black again. For a few moments, they just stared in silence at the tunnel.

"How are you doing, Harte?" Woolf asked at last. "You've not said much. I get it, you're nervous for him."

Blake nodded. "Oh, yeah. I am really nervous for him, there's no denying that. I don't think I've ever been more scared, if you want the truth. But I was just looking at the tunnel. I mean, really looking at it. How the hell did the Pennines disappear right in front of us like that?"

Woolf sighed. "You mind if I smoke?"

"Not if you give me one."

Woolf obliged and passed Blake a cigarette. He lit it with his clipper before placing the flame on his own and snapping the lid shut. "I dunno," he said as he inhaled. "I've seen a lot of weird, crazy stuff in my career. But a vanishing car, that's a new one on me."

"I mean, just cast your mind back to that night,"

Blake replied, as he gratefully blew the smoke out. It felt like the best one he had ever smoked in his entire life. "Pitch black, the rain lashing down, and a crazy guy behind the wheel of a car. There's nothing more dangerous."

"You got that right," replied Woolf.

"I mean, it's one of the first things we learn as a child, isn't it?" Blake continued, trying to keep his voice steady. "Never get into the car of a complete stranger if you don't know what their intentions are. But still, I went and did it, didn't I? My mother would have a fit if she found out."

Woolf took a long pull on his cigarette. "What's that supposed to mean?"

Blake kept staring straight ahead. "Oh, I think you know. You've known since the moment we met. Angel told me how brilliant your mind was, hell, *you* told me how brilliant your mind was. I didn't believe it at first." For some reason, Blake found himself laughing, though he did not feel in the slightest bit happy or amused. "I mean, I thought you were a complete idiot when I first met you."

Woolf nodded. "And now?"

Blake turned to him and smiled grimly. "Now? Oh, I still think you're an idiot. You've got to be. Anyone who takes drugs like you do has got to be an idiot. Reckless too. But I guess that's one of the signs."

Woolf stared at him. "Where do you get the idea

that I take drugs?"

"When I saw you yesterday at the B&B," Blake replied. "I'll admit, you're pretty good at hiding when you're high. You've learnt to be, I guess. The only thing you can't hide when you're on drugs though, no matter how good an actor you might be, you can't stop your eyes being the window to your soul. I think you got the cut of my mum pretty quickly. She probably couldn't tell a joint from a vitamin tablet, but me? I've been trained to notice these things and you knew that. Hence the sunglasses coming straight down over your eyes when you noticed me walking towards you so I wouldn't be able to see how large your pupils probably were." He flicked the cigarette out of the window. "It's a neat misdirection, but I'm afraid to say, not one I've never seen before."

Woolf chuckled as he blew out the smoke from his nose. "I see."

"Does it mean anything in the long run?" Blake continued lightly. "I mean, yeah, Angel finds out, he's the type to end your career there and then, but does you snorting your nose to pieces, or however you choose to partake, does it really mean anything on its own? Probably not. But then, this whole case started out with us after the Pennines, we've been after them for months. For what? Supplying. And who better to have on your side when you're trying to escape from the police than a bent copper? You've almost made me feel nostalgic, Alec, truly. I've not come across a bent copper since my days as a constable in Manchester. So, let's cut the crap, shall we? How long have you known Caroline Pennine? Truly?"

Woolf sighed. "You really think that I don't know that this is all some preamble to me spilling my guts to you while you've got your phone on record? Come on, Harte. Give me some credit."

Blake pulled a face and then produced his mobile from his pocket. "Why don't you give me some? I wouldn't insult you with child's play like that."

Woolf took Blake's phone out of his hand and examined it. When he was satisfied, he threw it over his shoulder into the back seat. Blake did not react, he merely waited for Woolf to begin.

"Sixteen years ago," Woolf said quietly. "Harmschapel is old news to me. It's just one of the places that I've been too. I've had a good life, Harte, I've travelled, I've seen things. I'm respected, admired even. There ain't many people that will say a bad word about me. Apart from Caroline, of course. She used to be a cop."

Blake stared at him in surprise. "You're kidding me. Caroline Pennine?"

"You're quick to judge, Harte, but believe it or not, she was going places. She was ambitious, she was brave, and she was absolutely smoking hot. Nobody could touch her. She could have had any man she wanted. She liked a bad boy though, which meant that I had to have her. You don't need to know the ins and outs, trust me, they're not important, but we began dating. And for a few months, everything was dandy. Then, I got itchy feet. I hadn't meant to stay around here for as long as I did, but she kind of had me in her grip. Then she told me she was pregnant. That was enough for me, so I left."

Blake stared at him. "Pregnant? Sixteen years ago? My God, you're James' dad, aren't you?"

"So she said," Woolf replied as he lit another cigarette, this time not offering Blake one. "But then she met Keith and told him that he was. To be honest, I was never sure that she wasn't dating us both at the same time, that's the kind of chick she was. The dates all matched. I even remember the night we did it, nine months before she gave birth. She had a good time that night."

Blake rolled his eyes. Even when he was finally telling the truth, Woolf was still as arrogant and irritating as ever. "So, what happened then? You found out she was pregnant with your child. Did you not want to stay and support her?"

Woolf scoffed. "No. Not at all. I don't care about kids, Harte. They change your life, and not for the better. You know what the collective term for a group of kids is? A migraine. A headache. A huge twenty year block in your life. I'm a free agent, always have been, always will be. I'm not even a cop, I'm a private detective. I kept hold of my ID for a bit of gravitas, but I haven't been a proper cop since I lived in the States. Seems that nobody told Angel that before he got in contact with me."

"And Angel got in touch with you to come help us in a case where the ultimate aim was to arrest your son?" Blake said, in disbelief. "Wow."

"I know, huh?" Woolf chuckled. "I'd have done it, like I say, I had no attachment to the kid. I've been paid for the work I've done here, now I can afford to take myself and this baby elsewhere." He patted the car's steering wheel fondly.

"If you cared so little about James, then why did you go to see him at the petrol station that day?" Blake asked. "I've got CCTV evidence and a witness confirming that you went in and asked for him."

Woolf stared into the distance. "He didn't know. As far as he was concerned, his dad was Keith. A waster, a slob, a cancer on his life. I guess I just wanted to see how he'd turned out. What can I say, I was high and got curious. It happens. Caroline knew that you guys were after him and Keith, and when she found out I was back, she took the opportunity to point out that she had more crap on me than anyone and said if I didn't help them, she'd hang me out to dry. They get away, they pay me some dollar, I still get paid here. It should have been a neat little transaction. That was until I realised one of the best detectives I've ever come across would probably have only had to have done a bit of his own digging before everything fell apart. I did my research on you. Hell, you were Thomas Frost's arresting officer, even I'd heard of him. One nasty serial killer. I knew we were going to have to come up with something pretty decent to buy the Pennines enough time to get away."

"So, you come up with the disappearing car trick," Blake said, nodding. "And I'll hand it to you, it stumped me. I mean really. Everything was just so perfect and impossible. And *that's* exactly where it fell apart. Too perfect. You and the Pennines rehearsed that chase to the letter. No matter how good a driver you are, these roads are treacherous. I mean, I've lived here long enough to know them, but even I get caught unawares on them sometimes. And yet, here you are, new to the area, able to zoom 'round them in this dinky little sports car, at night, in the middle of a cloudburst? No way. Everything that happened that night was perfected to the letter. The Pennines knew what they were doing, and you did too. You even knew what the weather would be doing, because you'd found out and timed it so you knew you'd be driving in it. The only person in the whole scenario who didn't have a clue was me. Even the type of car you used to chase them was relevant, actually, this car was the key to the whole thing, wasn't it?"

"You've worked it out?" Woolf exclaimed, clearly impressed. "Go on then. Amaze me."

Blake thought back to the night of the chase, making sure that all the pieces fit together. It still was all only a theory, but it was the only one that made sense. "When something big and senseless happens, sometimes you have to take it apart and look at the smaller aspects that don't fit. When we rammed into the back of their car, you said that your headlights had smashed, hence why they went out. So, how the hell do smashed headlights come back on to suddenly reveal that the car in front had mysteriously disappeared?" He studied Woolf's face, realising that he was right from the pained expression on his face. "They don't. Because they didn't smash at all. You and Keith had choreographed the whole thing too carefully for that. Your sports car has two sets of headlights. One set on the bottom and the other underneath those hoods. Hoods that lift up and reveal the lights. But the headlights aren't the vital thing here, it's the hoods themselves.

"When Keith slowed down to allow you to drive into the back of him, you both switched your lights off. Your front ones, and his back ones. In that few seconds of complete darkness, just before you entered the tunnel, he was free to quickly steer the car right where we're parked now. This passing spot. He never even entered the tunnel. We went in there all on our own. But, I credit myself with enough intelligence to say that I probably would have worked that out pretty quickly, I mean surely anybody would. So, you needed a little extra thing to convince me that we were still following the car when we went in the tunnel. That night, I was still looking at two red reverse lights in front of me. Just for a few seconds, because that's all it needed. I could be convinced that all the headlights were playing up because of the collision. You said you knew cars, and you do. You clearly have an exemplary knowledge of them, because you were able to get hold of some rear lights in the same shape as Keith's Accord Aerodeck. That's all you needed, just the lights. And that part happened before we even started chasing them. When we were walking towards the petrol station to apprehend them, you were behind me. It gave you enough time to stick the fake lights onto the back of the hoods on the headlights of your car. Everything happened so fast after that point and the rain was so heavy that I didn't even see them. When it all went dark after the impact and Keith had steered off the road, you just switched headlights from the bottom and raised the hoods up, switching the red lights on in the process. I'm now looking at a completely different set of lights to what I thought I was. Then you turn the red ones off, the headlights on, and all we've got in front of us is a clear road."

There was a pause, then Woolf slowly clapped.

"Bravo, Detective. You've got me fair and square."

Blake felt no satisfaction from working out the solution. He merely turned and looked straight at Woolf with a steely determination in his eyes. "Which just leaves me with two very important questions."

"Which are?"

"Number one – Who killed James Pennine and how? And then, number two, and I really, *really* need to know the answer to number two." He leant forwards so that he was just a couple of inches away from Woolf's face and spoke in a dangerous whisper. "*What have you done with my boyfriend, Woolf?*"

CHAPTER SIXTEEN

Woolf calmly finished his cigarette and chucked it out of the open window. Blake watched him, the fury still pounding through him.

"I gotta say," Woolf said at last. "You're good. I didn't expect you to work it all out."

"There's only one reason I know you're behind Harrison disappearing," Blake said, putting his hand in his pocket. "His phone was down the side of your passenger seat." He pulled Harrison's mobile out of his pocket and showed Woolf the screen.

Woolf stared at it for a few seconds and laughed. "Damn."

"Yeah," said Blake. "I just recorded you on this one instead. Harrison's phone isn't as good as mine, but it does the job. I've got all the evidence I need. So, I ask again. *Where – is – Harrison?*"

Woolf shrugged. "Fair enough. You got me. Excuse me." He leant across Blake and opened the glove compartment. Blake realised a second too late what he had retrieved from it as Woolf sharply pulled out a gun and pointed it at Blake. "Get out the car."

Blake stared at the gun for a moment, considering his options. "Woolf, don't be stupid."

The gun clicked in Woolf's hands as he prepared it to fire. "I said, get out the car."

With his mind racing, Blake slowly opened the car door and stepped out. The cold air immediately gripped him, but he barely noticed it as Woolf got out too, pointing the gun at him from across the roof of the car.

"Stay where you are," he said quietly. Without losing eye contact with Blake, Woolf moved to the back of the car and opened the boot. Blake watched him, wondering exactly what Woolf's plan was from here. Was he going to shoot Blake and make a run for it? Surely he knew that it would be obvious who Blake's killer would have been if he just vanished? But then, Woolf reached into the boot and grunted in effort as he pulled out what looked like a body, which crashed to the floor, out of Blake's sight. "Take a look," Woolf said calmly, holding the gun steadily at Blake.

Slowly, Blake walked to the back of the car and looked down at the body on the floor. When he saw who it was, he felt his heart skip a beat. "Harrison," Blake murmured. He stared at Woolf in fury. "What have you done to him?"

"Oh, stop whining, Harte," Woolf snapped. He leant down and picked up Harrison by the scruff of the neck, into a standing position. Harrison moaned weakly, his eyes fluttering. "Just a little knock out drug," Woolf said, seeming satisfied by the panic he could clearly see in Blake's face. "He'll be fine in a few hours. But that can soon change."

"Blake," Harrison murmured weakly. His eyes rolled to the back of his head as he slipped in and out of consciousness.

"He was in there the whole time?" Blake snapped furiously.

"Seems you two are pretty well matched," Woolf replied. "He can't keep his nose out of other people's business either. Now, walk. That way, go. And keep your hands where I can see them."

He waved the gun in the direction of the tunnel. Blake slowly put his hands up in the air and walked in the direction Woolf had indicated. As he made his way towards the tunnel, he could hear Harrison's feet being dragged across the ground.

"Up the footpath," Woolf snapped. "And don't try anything or your pretty little boyfriend gets a bullet in his brain."

"Okay, okay," Blake said quietly.

They walked up the path near the tunnel in silence. Blake was trying to work out exactly what Woolf had planned. Clearly, it had been his intention all along to get Blake on his own and Harrison was obviously going to be used as an incentive for him to do as Woolf told him, but he did not understand what the ultimate aim was.

They kept walking up the path, the car soon disappearing from view as the winding path took them further away from the road, until they eventually came to a river. The sound of the water flowing quickly along echoed around them.

"Stop there," Woolf ordered. Blake stopped, looking down at the dark water rushing beneath him. Woolf frogmarched Harrison to the edge of the river and held the gun straight at Blake.

"Now," he said quietly. "Here's what's going to happen. This river is pretty deep, and I don't think Harrison here is in any condition to swim, do you?"

Blake wanted nothing more than to rip Woolf apart with his bare hands, but he knew he had to be compliant for the moment, so just shook his head.

"So, it's simple," Woolf continued. "Show me that phone."

Blake reached slowly into his pocket and pulled out Harrison's phone, which was still recording. "Drop it in the river. Do it now."

Blake bit his lip, wondering if the recording could survive the water. Reluctantly, he held out his hand and dropped the phone. It landed in the river with a splash.

"Good boy," Woolf said. "Okay, so now you have a choice. I would honestly love to drop Harrison right in the water and watch you struggle to get him out with a bullet wound in your arm. After everything, it would give me so much pleasure, trust me. But I'm prepared to sacrifice my fun on one condition."

"And what's that?" Blake asked, watching him carefully.

"You let me go," Woolf replied simply. "You let me disappear and you'll never see me again. I take my money, and I go. No traps, no tricks. I'm out of this crummy village by morning and you make up some story to Angel."

"Like what?"

"You're a bright guy, Harte, I'm sure you'll think of something."

"You honestly expect me to let a murderer just go free?"

Woolf stared at him. "I haven't murdered

anyone."

"What about James Pennine? Or Keith? Come on, Woolf. There's nothing recording you now, you might as well tell me," Blake snapped.

"Harte, truthfully, I swear on my mother's life, I have no idea what happened to either of them. And I'm quite fond of my old mom. God bless her. I may be a lot of things, but I've never murdered anyone. So, do we have a deal?"

Blake looked down at the river. "Even if I choose to believe you, you think I'm just going to let you run off into the sunset after everything you've done? Abducting *my* boyfriend? Helping two suspects to escape? Taking drugs while on the job? I don't think so."

Woolf chuckled and held Harrison's limp body over the river. "Admirable work ethic, Harte, but I don't see how you've got a huge amount of choice."

Blake's heart hammered in his chest. The only way he could see out of this was to call Woolf's bluff. "Don't you? I do. Go on then, drop him in and shoot me. You just said yourself, you're no murderer. Arrogant, a complete arsehole, but you haven't got in you to murder anyone."

Woolf stared at him in disbelief. There was a long pause. Blake could see him weighing up his options.

"Well," he said quietly. "There's a first time for everything."

And everything seemed to go in slow motion. Woolf released his grip on Harrison and he plunged into the river.

"*Harrison!*" yelled Blake, rushing forwards to grab him.

"Big mistake, Harte!" snarled Woolf. He pointed the gun straight at Blake's chest and pulled the trigger. Blake shielded threw his arms up and waited for the bullet to hit him.

Nothing happened.

Blake looked up at Woolf who was staring at his gun in furious confusion. He pulled the trigger again but it just clicked pointlessly in his hand.

"I believe you're looking for these, Detective Woolf," came a voice behind them.

It was Angel. He was holding a bullet in one hand and what looked like a remote control in the other. "I found them when I was admiring your car," he said, walking towards them. "I've never been much of a fan of firearms. I was going to call you to my office and condescend you into telling me why you own a gun, but I suppose this works just as well."

He lifted the device he was holding up at Woolf and pressed a button. As Woolf suddenly cried out in pain, Blake realised that it was a taser. Woolf collapsed on the ground, convulsing in agony.

"DS Harte, I believe the love of your life has just been thrown in a river, so I suggest you get him out,"

Angel replied, holding the taser steady on Woolf's twitching body.

Blake did not need telling twice. He dived into the river, and the freezing cold water immediately almost made him gasp once submerged. He opened his eyes and looked frantically around. The river was murky, and it was almost impossible to see anything in the dark, but then, Blake saw Harrison. He was lying on the river's bed, completely still. With all the effort he could muster, Blake dived down to the bottom and grabbed Harrison's arm. His leg was caught in a mass of weeds sticking out of the mud, and try as he might, Blake could not pull him free. Fully aware of how much time Harrison had been submerged, Blake desperately pulled his head towards him and placed his lips over Harrison's mouth, blowing as much oxygen into him as he could, whilst attempting to wrench his leg free. At last, with a barely audible sucking sound, Harrison's leg was released from the weeds and together, they floated up to the surface of the water, just as Blake's head was becoming almost too light to cope with his own lack of air. They broke the surface of the water and Blake gasped, filling his lungs with some well needed oxygen.

A hand grabbed his shoulder and pulled him to the river's edge. Gasping for breath, Blake looked up to see Gardiner, hauling him back up on the bank again. "There's an ambulance on its way," he said. "We called it just in case once we saw Woolf walking you towards here with a gun. It'll be here any moment."

Blake barely heard him. Once he and Harrison were out of the water, he got on his knees and listened for Harrison breathing. He heard nothing, so immediately blew into his mouth before beginning to pump his chest thirty times. Then, four more breaths into his mouth.

As he frantically began pumping Harrison's chest again, the sound of an ambulance siren wailing could be heard echoing in the distance.

"Sergeant Gardiner," Blake heard Angel say. "Go and get them."

"Come *on,* Harrison," Blake cried as he frantically tried to pump life back into Harrison's limp and unresponsive body. "Don't you *dare.*"

Soon, he felt another set of hands pull him away and then, two paramedics were on Harrison, resuming Blake's action. After what seemed like hours, pumping his chest, Harrison began to cough.

"*Oh,*" Blake exclaimed, his eyes immediately filling with relieved tears.

"Okay, get him on the stretcher," one of the paramedics ordered the other. He looked up at Blake. "He's swallowed a lot of water, but once we get him in the ambulance, I think he's going to be alright."

Blake nodded, shivering with either cold or fear, he wasn't sure which. "Thank you."

***

As Harrison was taken to the ambulance, wrapped tightly in blankets, Blake himself was checked over by another paramedic. "I'm fine," Blake insisted.

"Of course you are," Angel said from behind him. "I feel I owe you an apology, DS Harte. I can't help but feel entirely responsible for this whole affair. If I hadn't brought Alec Woolf here, young Harrison would not be where he is right now."

Blake had not considered that viewpoint, and for a few moments was angry with Angel, but then realised that he had also saved both his and Harrison's life. "You removed his bullets. I think that makes up for it."

"Well, yes," Angel said. "I had a phone call. From a Sergeant Sally-Ann Matthews. She was trying to find senior officers who had worked with Woolf in the past. The questions she was asking, I could not help but wonder if Woolf was really everything I thought he was. Then, when I found that gun, I knew I had a problem on my hands. Once he had driven you off, I followed with Sergeant Gardiner. There's certainly something to be gained from turning off your headlights when pursuing somebody."

"We still don't know what happened to James Pennine," Blake said quietly. "Or where Keith is."

"With an officer of your calibre, I fail to see how those questions will remain unanswered for long," Angel replied, placing a hand on Blake's shoulder. He looked up at the ambulance. "Ah, I think they're ready to go. The NHS, wonderful service. I'll see you back at the station when you get out of the hospital. No hurry."

Blake nodded and climbed into the ambulance. Just before the doors closed, he could see Woolf being led to the back of the police car, which was parked not far from the passing spot where the silver sports car was stood.

Gripping Harrison's hand, Blake sat down as the doors slammed shut and they were driven to the hospital.

ROBERT INNES

CHAPTER
SEVENTEEN

The next morning, Blake arrived back at the station. He had not had a wink of sleep, but he did not feel in the slightest bit tired. All through the night, the doctors and nurses had treated Harrison and were confident that he was going to make a full recovery, though they wanted to keep him in for a couple more days. As Blake had left, one doctor had told him that Harrison had been incredibly lucky. Blake could not help but agree with him.

"Ah, DS Harte," Angel said as Blake walked into

the meeting room to tumultuous applause from the rest of the team. "Perfect timing. How is young Mr Baxter?"

"He's going to be fine," Blake said. "He's asleep at the moment, while whatever drug Woolf gave him works its way through his body."

"Excellent," Angel replied.

"That's great news, Sir," Patil agreed. "We were just about to go and search that house. The one we found James Pennine in. Now we haven't got Woolf breathing down our necks and leading us astray, we might actually find some answers."

"I'm no use at the hospital," Blake said. "I'll come with you."

"Are you sure you're up to it, Sir?" Mattison asked him. "You must have been up all night?"

"I'll be alright. Somebody's got to keep you in order, Matti," Blake grinned. "Come on."

***

When they arrived at the house, Caroline was waiting for them. She looked like she had actually had a bath, and smelt a lot more pleasant that the last time Blake had seen her.

"Alright?" she said as the team pushed past her and into the house. "Mr Harte, can I talk to ya?"

Blake nodded and walked with her towards the

cellar. "I was talking to Alec Woolf last night," he told her. "He told me about how you met, and that he was probably James' father?"

Caroline leant against the cellar wall. "Yeah," she said. "He rang me last night. I was his phone call. Can you believe that?"

"What did he say?"

Caroline smirked. "He was going on about how I could get him out of prison if I told all these lies. Make a load of stuff up, say that Keith had been back in touch, and had forced him into helpin' me or some crap."

"And what did you say?" Blake asked her.

"I 'ung up," Caroline replied. "I'm sick of men tellin' me what to do. With James gone, I don't even care anymore. The last time I saw Keith, I told him. He's a nasty man. I used to be someone, I used to have a life."

"Woolf told me," Blake replied. "You used to be an officer?"

Caroline snorted. "Yeah, that was before I met Keith. I dunno how he did it, but he ground me down, y'know? Before I knew it, I was some yes woman to a guy who was making all his money from dealing drugs. I used to arrest scum like him. But then, my career ended and I found meself bringin' up a kid with only dirty money to feed him on. When Alec turned back up out of the blue, I decided I was done lying. I told Keith that James wasn't his. He was just about to go and pick him up from work. The night we pulled off that disappearing car thing. He was fumin'. I guess you can understand why, but that was the last time I saw him. He just left me, without another word. I don't think he even knows James is dead. So, I don't owe him nothin' now."

She took a deep breath. Blake could see glimpses of a once strong, independent woman, that was trying to come out again. "He hid all his drugs under the floor in that cellar."

Blake looked inside the cellar and at the wooden planks on the floor.

"That's why we got this place," Caroline told him. "Out in the middle of nowhere, somewhere to 'ide all his stuff. And he's got a list of numbers too. Dealers, customers, suppliers."

Blake called the officers over and they began prying open the wooden slates in the cellar. Soon, they had discovered an enormous stash of class A drugs – cocaine, ecstasy, MDMA, amphetamines, heroin, and underneath one of the bags, a small black book containing an array of contact details for people that Blake had seen under the most wanted list since he had arrived in Harmschapel. He walked across the cellar as the team continued retrieving the supplies from the ground.

"Wow," he said as one officer produced a large bag

full of white tablets. "There must be thousands of pounds worth of gear here. Let's try and keep the press away from this. You know what they're like."

Caroline watched from the doorway as they continued retrieving the buried goods from underneath the floorboards. Then, Blake leant down and pulled up another floorboard on the other side of the cellar. Underneath was a hole that looked much deeper than the rest of the cellar. As he continued pulling the floor up, he suddenly gasped and recoiled. A cold, lifeless face was staring back at him. Blake gaped at it as he began pulling the rest of the floorboards up around him with a crowbar. Soon, a whole body was visible beneath him. It was Keith Pennine.

"Guys," Blake murmured as the rest of the team gathered round. "Call Sharon." Clutched in Keith's hand was another needle. "I think we might just have found James' killer."

ROBERT INNES

ONE WEEK LATER

Harrison shook his head in disbelief as he began putting all his toiletries into his bag, which was lying on the hospital bed. He had finally been discharged and was feeling better than he had done all week. "So, you think he killed his son?"

Blake shrugged. "It wasn't his son. Caroline said he was a nasty piece of work. She told him that Woolf was James' father. Once they'd burnt that car out, and I'm just guessing here, they must have walked across to the house. Sharon said that Keith's body was wrecked on the inside. If corpses could be high, Keith would have been having the time of his life underneath those floorboards. That needle he had clutched in his hand had James' DNA on it as well as his. Maybe they went back to that cellar, argued, and Keith in some sort of drugged up fuelled rage injected him."

"Why hang him though?" Harrison asked, mystified.

"Who knows?" Blake replied, shaking his head. "Maybe he wanted to hurt Caroline as much as she'd hurt him. Make it look as though James thought he had nothing to live for. Once he had James' body hanging from the roof of the cellar, he must have decided to just top himself. He made himself a little grave, covered himself with the floorboards, then injected himself. I mean there was enough drugs in that cellar to fill an entire factory."

Harrison exhaled in amazement. "So, someone did commit suicide in there?"

"Yep," replied Blake. "But it wasn't who we were supposed to think it was." He stood up from his chair. "Anyway, enough of that. Let's get you home. Have you got everything?"

"Yeah," Harrison replied. He had done a mental list of the few things Blake had brought him to keep him entertained and had managed to fit it all into one bag. It had been nice doing nothing for a few days, but after a week, even the good-looking porter was not enough to stop him from wanting to escape.

"Come on then," Blake said, holding his hand. Together, they thanked the staff and set off down the corridor. "You know," said Blake. "I was scared when I pulled you out of that river. I genuinely thought I'd lost you."

Harrison squeezed his hand. "In the time we've known each other, you've saved me from being pushed off a church roof, almost being struck by lightning in the process, saved me from drowning, and I've also survived your mother giving me the tenth degree. I think it's fair to say, I'm here to the long run."

Blake grinned and kissed him. "You better be."

***

The lift doors slid open and standing in front of them were Blake's parents.

"What are you doing here?" Blake asked them worriedly. "Mum, don't give Harrison a hard time, please, not right now."

"Blake," Stephanie said sternly, glaring at her son over her glasses. "I wouldn't dream of it. If everything happened the way you said it did, then I am standing in front of possibly the bravest boy I ever met in my life." She pushed a bag of grapes she was carrying into Blake's arms, then grabbed Harrison and gripped him in a tight hug.

"Aye," said Colin. "And she had something else

she wanted to say to, didn't you?" Stephanie stuttered. "*Didn't you?*" repeated Colin.

"Yes," Stephanie replied quietly. "I suppose I did. Harrison, I'm sorry. I was cold, I was unfeeling, and I was wrong. I should never have treated you this way. I can see now that Blake is absolutely enamoured by you, and as long as my son is happy, then that is all I can ask for. I just wanted to say that before we left."

"You're leaving?" Blake asked. Harrison glanced at him. He was unsure as to whether Blake looked more relieved or sad.

"Yes," Stephanie replied. "Oh don't worry, we'll be back to see you more often."

"Oh," Blake said weakly. "Good."

"Aye," Colin added. "Me and this lad here have got beer to drink in that pub. What do you reckon, Harrison? Couple of pints with the in-law?"

"Sounds good to me," Harrison grinned.

"But, before we go," Stephanie said, straightening her collar. "I would love it if we could have a family meal. Just the four of us."

"Four?" Blake repeated, winking at Harrison. "You mean, Harrison too?"

"Of course," Stephanie said sharply. "Harrison is a part of this family, now isn't he?" She gripped Harrison by the arm and led him towards the lift. "He does have a tendency to get a little jealous sometimes," she murmured to him. "But we can sort that out, can't we? Together."

Harrison looked back at Blake. "Yeah. I reckon so."

The four of them entered the lift. As Blake and Stephanie began squabbling about who was going to hold the grapes that she had brought, it was music to Harrison's ears. Finally, he thought as the lift doors slid shut, he had his own family again.

ROBERT INNES

To keep up to date with **Robert Innes'** future releases, follow him on **Facebook** at:

facebook.com/RobertInnesAuthor

Printed in Great Britain
by Amazon